ZANE

BAYOU CRESCENT WOLVES

BOOK ONE

BY MADISON GRANGER

Zane, Bayou Crescent Wolves

By Madison Granger

Table of Contents

Dedication

To the ones who continue to support me.

Acknowledgements

Betty Shreffler of BJR Cover Designs
I fell in love with Zane's cover the moment I saw
it. I'm looking forward to the completed trilogy.

Sandy Ebel of Personal Touch Editing
The woman who continues to polish all my
rough edges, making my stories shine with a
magic of their own.

Kristy Cobb
For sharing knowledge of her Native American
heritage and teaching me about the United
Houma Nation, once known as the Ouma tribe,
traiteurs, and healers.

Chapter 1

"You're actually going to do this?" Amber stopped midstride, a hand on her hip, as she shot Zane an incredulous look.

"What? Are you kidding me?" Zane ran a hand through his short black hair, tugging at the ends in frustration. "We've been through this. You didn't want to stay with the Crossroads pack, and you've done nothing but cause trouble in Bayou Crescent. This is your only option, Amber." He glared at her until she dropped her gaze. "You agreed to the transfer. It's too late to turn back now."

Amber eased up to him, her hand trailing up his arm. She bit her bottom lip, giving him a pleading look with large, dark brown eyes.

"I always thought you and I would hook up."

"You knew better than that from the start." Zane closed his eyes, praying for patience. "You're not my Fated Mate, and I don't play those games." He moved away from her touch and gestured toward the two-story, rustic office. "Come on, the Alpha is waiting for us, and I, for one, don't plan on making him angry."

With a long-suffering sigh, Amber walked alongside him. Zane opened the door, and she strode past him, throwing herself onto a chair. Rolling his eyes, Zane ignored her and made his way to the receptionist, introducing himself and stating their business. Within minutes, they were shown to a large, masculine office.

Steven Woodward sat behind a polished antique walnut desk. Opened books stacked atop one another took up more than half of the available space, leaving barely enough room for the computer and phone. As they entered, the Alpha rose, skirting the desk to warmly shake Zane's hand.

"My apologies for not being here yesterday to greet you. Pack business had me out of town longer than I anticipated. I hope your accommodations were to your satisfaction?"

"No apology is necessary. Pack business is priority." A look of understanding passed between them. "Your staff saw to our every need and comfort. I wish I had more time to visit. I'd like to discuss your secret of keeping everything so organized, especially in your absence."

"Careful selection and loyalty." Steven chuckled under his breath. "It wasn't always this way. It's taken me years to reach this level of trust and management." He glanced at Amber, who was fixedly staring out the window. "I assume this is our new member?"

"Amber." Zane's jaw clenched when the female refused to acknowledge him.

A wave of power charged the air, and Amber whined, baring her neck in submission. Zane felt the power, but being an alpha himself, didn't feel the impulse to submit.

"Amber Gardner, your acceptance into this pack hinges on your respect, adherence to the laws I lay down, and your submission. Do you understand?" The pack leader's eyes glowed a brilliant gold, his voice a low growl filling the room with authority.

"Yes, Alpha, I understand." A sheen of perspiration covered the omega's face, her hands clenching the arms of the chair. She gasped, slumping back in the chair when Steven pulled in his power, releasing her from its hold.

Woodward nodded in satisfaction, turning his attention back to Zane.

"She'll be fine. Once she's settled and acquainted with our ways, we'll find her a suitable job, and she'll become a contributing pack member."

Zane didn't miss the shocked look in Amber's eyes and bit back harsh laughter. The omega was in for a rude awakening, and he was sorry he wouldn't be there to see it.

"Thank you for helping us out." Zane shook Steven's hand firmly. "If it wouldn't have been for Maddox steering us in your direction..."

"Don't worry about it." The Denver Alpha leaned in closer and whispered in Zane's ear. "I've had a fair amount of experience with this kind of problem. She's better off here."

The knowing look in Woodward's eyes settled any misgivings Zane had about dumping the omega onto another pack.

Turning, Zane caught Amber's gaze, raking him up and down, her dark eyes smoldering and a wicked tongue licking her full, ripe lips. He frowned as he walked out of the Denver pack leader's office. The she-wolf didn't get it... she would, though, soon enough.

Amber had been one of a dozen or more omegas who had been abused by their pack alpha. Rescued by Rafe Martin, leader of the Crossroads pack, Amber had swiftly realized the fit wasn't a good one in the family-oriented clan and had asked to be allowed to join the Bayou Crescent wolves. It hadn't taken Zane or his brothers long to figure out there was no pack in Louisiana who would ever satisfy Amber. Even though she was an omega, she was restless and prone to drama, stirring up trouble on a daily basis.

Thanks to Maddox Ward, Alpha of the NOLA Shifters and his network of packs in the U.S., he'd been able to set up the transfer for Amber to move to Denver. Their pack was larger than all the packs in Louisiana put together, and Amber would have her choice of unmated males to play with. As long as she didn't play her games with the mated ones, she'd be fine.

If she kept up her little tricks, however, she'd find herself up against an alpha who brooked no tolerance with troublesome omegas. If Amber didn't toe the line here, she'd find herself packless... and even she knew the consequences of such a fate.

Striding across the parking area to his rental, Zane felt a sense of relief this was finally behind him. His timing couldn't have been more perfect. By the time he got to the airport, he wouldn't have long to wait for his flight. He wasn't crazy about flying, not many shifters were. He would have preferred to make the trip to Denver on his bike, regardless of the distance, but there was no way he would go anywhere with Amber clutched to his backside. She would have taken full advantage of the situation and no doubt, they would have ended up wrecked somewhere between Louisiana and Colorado. The flight was a no-brainer.

Once on the plane, Zane pulled out a paperback he'd bought at the airport on the trip in. Figuring if his nose was buried in a book, Amber would leave him alone. The ruse had worked, for the most part. When she realized he wasn't going to talk to her more than what was necessary, she'd resorted to watching a movie on her tablet.

His choice of book was regrettable, but he was committed to it, and had started reading. The picture of a wolf on the cover had caught his eye. He'd picked it up without skimming the synopsis on the back cover, much less paying attention to the title. Turned out, it was one of the paranormal romances that seemed to be all the rage these days.

Since he was already more than halfway through the story, he figured he'd might as well finish it. It wasn't a horrible book, just not accurate. What shifter story would be? Their secret was top priority and would remain that way for the unforeseeable future.

"Are you enjoying the book?" The low-pitched, provocative voice held more than a hint of humor.

Zane looked up to find the flight attendant smiling at him, her eyes dancing with mirth. Heat coursed up his neck, and he fingered the collar of his shirt.

"Not my usual read. I picked it up by accident." He shrugged, a corner of his mouth tugging into a smile. "I was bored, figured I'd give it a shot."

"It's actually a rather good story." She winked at him, openly flirting. "The author is one of my favorites. You should read some of her other works."

"Um, yeah, I'll look into it." *That would be a definite no.*

"Is there anything I can get for you?" The attendant leaned over him, giving him a view of generous breasts straining against the fabric of her uniform.

"No, I'm fine. Thanks." Zane had nowhere to go. She was practically on top of him, and her perfume was speedily giving him a headache. "It's a short flight. I'm good."

She unhurriedly straightened as she made one last attempt.

"If you change your mind, my name is Carol."

"Appreciate it." Zane waved the book and winked at her. "Need to finish this before we land."

With a smile, she moved on to check on the other passengers.

Zane leaned against the seat, breathing easier now she was gone. The flight attendant was an attractive woman, and no doubt, he could have spent a few hours of pleasure with her, but she wasn't his type, and he had other things on his mind than a quick dalliance with a human.

Opening the paperback, he made himself focus on the pages, blocking out the passengers around him and the fact he was in a metal can flying way too high above the ground.

When the landing announcement came, Zane closed the book with a snap, tossing it on the empty seat beside him. He'd finished it, but would leave it for someone else to pass the time.

Zane wasted no time, grabbing his carry-on and heading for the garage parking lot. Not having luggage to claim saved him aggravation, and he started up the black Ford Raptor with a grunt of satisfaction. The roar of the engine echoing in the enclosed area, he eased out of the parking bay, making his way to the highway and home.

Squinting against the harsh sunlight, Zane slipped on his aviator sunglasses and kicked on the air conditioning. It would take a few minutes before the air cooled, but it would be worth the wait. Summer in south Louisiana was always a scorcher, and while he was used to the heat and humidity, he'd be lying if he said he didn't appreciate air conditioning.

Zane tapped a button on the steering wheel. "Call Ridge," he growled at the voice-activated multimedia system. He may have been raised down in the bayou, living a simple life, but he did love technology and all the gadgets that came with it.

"Made it back in one piece, brother?" Ridge's soft Cajun cadence was a balm to Zane's ears. His ties to Bayou Crescent and his brothers were strong, and Zane was more at peace when he was home.

"Yeah, I'm on Highway 90. Should be there in an hour or so."

"Good deal. Try to avoid any more speeding tickets." Ridge sniggered, knowing darn well Zane had a heavy foot, especially since he'd bought the new truck. "Everything go okay in Denver?"

"As well as could be expected. We owe Maddox a big favor, though. You know that, right?"

Zane waited patiently for his brother's response. Ridge weighed each word before he spoke. Some saw it as a flaw or defect until he said his piece. Ridge wasn't slow—he was careful.

"I know, and it's been discussed. I'll take care of it when it's time."

Zane knew better than to press him. Ridge would talk when he was good and ready, and only if he thought Zane needed to know.

"You always do, bro. I'm going to duck off and grab some lunch at Sparh's before I head home. I missed breakfast and my stomach is rumbling." The popular seafood restaurant was in a prime location between Bayou Crescent and New Orleans, on a stretch of highway with no competitors nearby.

"Order a takeout for me and Cole," Ridge requested, a hint of laughter in the deep rumble. "I could go for a seafood platter."

"If you'd get out of the bayou once in a while, you could try some of these restaurants."

"Why? You're there already. Bring some home. Drive carefully, Zane."

The line went dead, and Zane snorted. Typical Ridge.

An hour later, his belly full, and the truck smelling like all kinds of seafood heaven, thanks to the two large to-go bags on the floorboard, Zane eased back onto the highway. A nap sounded better than the drive home, but he'd wasted enough time and was eager to get back to Bayou Crescent.

Chapter 2

Zane twisted the cap off the bottle of beer and took a long pull. The cold, golden brew felt good going down, and he felt the tension between his shoulders ease.

"That she-wolf really did a number on you." Cole smirked as he helped himself to a beer.

"She was relentless. As many times as I told her no, you would have thought she'd get the message and give up, but she's a new breed of persistent."

"Amber had you pegged from the get-go." Cole snorted. "Even I couldn't get her attention, and that's saying something."

"True enough." Zane laughed easily at his brother's statement.

The brothers ragged Cole about being the pack's man-whore, but it was only meant as a good-natured joke. The youngest of the Landry brothers loved females, shifters and humans both, and they loved him right back, even knowing about his roving eyes and philandering ways. With dark auburn hair, brilliant green eyes, and a killer smile, Cole never had trouble attracting the opposite sex. It was part of his charm, and Cole used it to his advantage.

Zane, on the other hand, was selective and discreet. Not looking for anything permanent, he treated his lovers with respect and a gentle hand. Deep down, he always hoped he'd find his Fated Mate. He wanted the kind of soul-binding love his parents had known and didn't want to settle for anything less.

The back door opened and closed quickly before the summer heat found its way inside the dim coolness of the bar. Ridge Landry silently padded to the front, acknowledged his brothers, and scanned the empty room all in a glance.

"You good?" Ridge asked Zane, alert hazel eyes taking in the near-empty bottle he held.

"Yeah, now that I got that mess behind us, I can breathe a little easier." Zane pointed at the small stage where a band would be setting up for the evening. "It's going to be a good night. Hopefully, things can get back to normal."

Friday and Saturday nights at The Den were always busy. The small community of Bayou Crescent liked to blow off steam after working all week, gathering to drink, shoot pool, or play a round of darts. Over the years, various supernaturals, commonly referred to as Otherkind, had found their way to The Den, making it their favorite hangout. Standing rule was no display of powers since a few humans occasionally showed up, enjoying the relaxed ambiance of the country bar.

There wasn't much else to do unless you wanted to make the drive into Bellerieve. The mid-sized city held various restaurants and nightclubs for entertainment and pleasure. Considering the entire settlement of Bayou Crescent comprised wolf shifters, they tended to keep to themselves, preferring their home turf.

The Bayou Crescent wolves were led by the Landry brothers, and Zane was second born and Beta of the pack. His older brother, Ridge, was Alpha, and Cole, the baby... Zane snorted. Cole, at six foot three and rock solid, was the pack's Enforcer. Many had underestimated the brothers because they led a small pack, calling the deep bayou of Louisiana their home. They didn't realize until they came face-to-face with the brothers that the Landry men were all alphas, no matter the positions they held.

"I could use a little normal." Ridge agreed, brushing unruly hair from his face. The Alpha wore his dark hair longer than his brothers, mostly because he couldn't be bothered with setting up appointments for haircuts.

"We're on the same page, bro." Zane tipped his bottle toward his brother. "Ever since the Plantation pack went to shit, there's always some kind of drama finding their way to all the packs."

Months ago, drug suppliers had insinuated their way into several of the Louisiana packs, distributing a drug called Moonburst. The Plantation Alpha and his highest ranked males had rapidly become addicted, physically abusing their omegas during marathon orgies. Rafe Martin, leader of the Crossroads pack, had rescued the omegas and eradicated the Alpha and others, then turned to all the pack alphas in the state for aid in getting rid of the drug.

"Until we get a handle on Moonburst, we can expect trouble. Maddox sent a team up to Chicago to check out the vamp, Thaddeus Holloway. His club, Sanction Noir, is a hot bed for sex and drug trafficking."

"So, we stay on high alert in the meantime?"

Ridge nodded in agreement. "Even tucked away in the bayou, we're not guaranteed immunity. We need to remain vigilant."

"Luckily for us, outsiders tend to stick out like a sore thumb if they make it this far down the highway."

"True enough," Ridge agreed. "C'mon Cole, let's unload those cases and get the place stocked before the crowd gets here." Ridge glanced at Zane. "You got this?"

Zane looked around the empty bar and grinned.

"Yeah, I think I can handle it. Make sure you have a couple of extra kegs on hand. With a band playing, the guys will be bringing their mates. It'll get rowdy by ten."

"Got you covered. We'll stock up, then come back around nine."

"Sounds good. Catch y'all later." Zane grabbed a handful of quarters from a jar under the bar and strode over to the jukebox. Picking his favorites, he sang along softly when the first song started playing. Wandering around the room, he straightened chairs and made sure the place was ready for the evening.

He was going over an order when the door opened, daylight slashing through the dim bar.

Zane glanced at the clock on the wall. It was only six, too early for his regular crowd.

The woman was stunning—tall and curvy in all the right places, with long, chestnut waves of hair falling around her shoulders and down her back. Her dark eyes sparkled as her lips curved into a smile.

"Hello. Is your boss around?"

"That would be me." He extended a hand as she approached the bar. "Zane Landry. How can I help you?"

"Calista Evans, but everyone calls me Callie. I was wondering if you were hiring? I'm experienced and have references."

She looked him straight in the eye as she was speaking, her voice low and smoky, which Zane found more than appealing. When she leaned forward to take his hand, the scent of orange blossoms assaulted his senses. His wolf appeared from the void, alert and watching.

"You're a long way from anywhere to be job hunting, Callie." Zane crossed his arms over his chest as he studied the gorgeous female. Ridge's warning to remain vigilant was foremost in his mind, but her scent called to him... his wolf was intrigued, too. There was something else, but he couldn't pin it down. "How did you find your way down here?"

"I was in New Orleans last week and ran into an old friend, Bishop Callan. He said you knew him, and he would put in a good word for me."

Zane's eyes narrowed at the mention of Maddox Ward's Beta. He knew Bishop,—they all did, a white tiger shifter and a formidable opponent. On a positive note, Bishop was friends with the Landry's, but how did Callie tie in with him?

"I could use another bartender, especially on the weekends. How soon can you start?"
Ridge would have his head for not running this by him first, but Zane couldn't let Callie walk out that door. He needed to keep her close—something he couldn't begin to explain.

"I could start tonight." Callie grinned, excitement lighting up her face. "Is there a motel around here? It's a long drive back to Bellerieve."

"Afraid not. Bayou Crescent isn't even a ding on the map, but I might be able to swing something temporarily until you can find a place to rent." He couldn't believe the words rolling out of his mouth. Had he lost his damn mind? Ridge would be positive that was the case. "I'll take you over there when we close. It's furnished... pots, pans, towels, and linens. You'll need to pick up groceries, but you can get almost anything at the store you passed getting here."

"Sounds like a dream come true. Thanks. You have no idea how much I appreciate this."

"Don't thank me too fast." Zane grabbed a towel and tossed it to her, gesturing toward the racks of glasses needing to be wiped down. "I still need to call Bishop and run this by my brothers. I'm not your only boss," he smirked.

"Bishop filled me in on you and your brothers. Ridge is the oldest and Alpha, you're the Beta, and Cole is the Enforcer."

"Well, that's the basics." Zane grinned.

The back door opened, and two women walked in.

"Kitty, Destiny, come up here a sec." As they approached, Zane made the introductions. "I want y'all to meet Callie Evans. She's going to be our new bartender. Callie, this is Kitty and Destiny. They serve drinks and keep everyone in line."

Zane didn't miss the questioning looks the waitresses gave him, but they were polite to Callie. He was grateful for that much, knowing he would have to fill them in quickly. As a rule, they hired pack, not total strangers who literally walked in off the street.

"Why don't you ladies show Callie where she can stash her purse and where everything is? I need to make a couple of quick calls." Turning to Callie, he added, "I'll be in my office if you need anything."

Easing behind the battered oak desk, Zane dialed Ridge's cell phone. He would get enough grief from his older brother. There was no sense in putting it off any longer.

"What's up?"

"I hired a bartender."

The silence on the line was predictable. Ridge was a man of few words, and he thought carefully before he spoke.

"You don't need my permission, so I'm assuming there's more to this."

"She's not pack." Zane held his breath a beat, then laid out the rest. "Her name is Callie Evans. She walked in and asked if we were hiring."

"Have you lost your damn mind?" Ridge growled. "Didn't we have this conversation literally an hour ago?"

"I know, but there's more to it."

"This better be good," Ridge demanded.

"Bishop Callan sent her." Zane leaned back, the rolling chair creaking as his weight shifted. "She needs a place to stay, so I'm giving her my place for now. If she works out, I'll find her a place to rent somewhere close."

"Seems like you jumped in with both feet, brother. I hope you know what you're doing."

"Me too. There's something about her. I need to figure it out, and it'll be easier if she's close at hand."

"I trust your judgement. I only hope she's not packing trouble." Ridge let out a long breath. "She's your responsibility, so keep an eye on her. I'm gonna call Bishop and get the story on her. What's her name again?"

"Calista Evans. She goes by Callie."

Chapter 3

Six hours later, Zane had zero regrets about hiring Callie Evans. She hadn't been lying about being experienced. Once she had the layout of the place and was briefed on drink prices and who had tabs, she was off and running. She fit in easily, and the crowd readily accepted her. When things got crazy, as they usually did after ten, Ridge, Callie, and Zane worked the bar together flawlessly.

He still needed to know a lot more about Callie, but it would come in time. They'd been slammed with customers and Zane hadn't had a chance to talk to Ridge about Bishop. He'd have to wait until they went home to find out what the NOLA Beta had to say about Callie.

By the time three o'clock rolled around, Kitty and Destiny were nursing drinks and sore feet. They hadn't stopped for breaks and were exhausted. Zane and Ridge were stacking chairs on the tables while Cole swept the floors around them, and Callie filled the dishwasher with the remainder of the evening's glasses.

"That's a wrap." Zane took stock of the room, nodding in satisfaction. "Go home and get some rest. We'll do it again tonight."

"If this keeps up, I'm going to want a raise." Kitty rolled her eyes.

"Me, too," Destiny chimed in.

They both eyed Callie, who held her hands up in surrender.

"I barely started. I don't even know what the pay is."

"She didn't fill out any paperwork either, I bet." Ridge glared at Zane.

"My bad. I'll fill her in on all the rest tonight before work." Zane winked at Callie. "I got sidetracked."

"I bet you did." Cole snorted.

"On that note, unless you people want to spend the night here, I suggest you head for the parking lot. I'm locking up," Zane announced.

Apparently, Ridge had passed on to Cole that the new female was, for the time being, Zane's responsibility and not to be messed with. Cole had not been anything except friendly and cordial, which was a relief for Zane. He didn't want trouble with either of his brothers, especially over a female.

"Where are you parked?" Zane asked Callie.

"Out front."

"My truck is in the back. I'll walk you to your car and you can drive around back, then follow me."

Stepping outside, a lone, dark red car sat in the parking lot.

"Is that... " Zane peered into the darkness, then strode toward the vehicle. "It's a Hellcat."

"My pride and joy." Callie laughed low. "Meet Jett." She pushed on a fob, unlocking the doors.

"Jett, huh?" Zane asked as he eased onto the passenger seat.

"Yeah, she's so fast you feel like you're flying," Callie said with pride, patting the dashboard. The engine rumbled and Callie eased the car around to the back of the building, with Zane guiding the way.

"We'll be at the cabin in five minutes," Zane told her as he slipped out of the Challenger and headed to his truck. The Raptor roared to life, and

Callie fell in behind him as he navigated the roads leading home.

Passing the two-story Craftsman house that had been their parent's home and was now officially Ridge's, Zane drove deeper into the woods. On his left was Cole's cabin, surrounded in darkness. His own place would be the same.

Years ago, Ridge had been mated and Zane and Cole had built their own homes farther into the forest. When his mate died tragically, the brothers had moved back into the family home in an effort to keep their older brother and Alpha grounded to family and pack. It had been rough for several years, but they'd managed to get through it. Ridge still grieved for his mate, always would, but he stayed for the pack's sake, and the brothers never left the family home, leaving their own cabins empty.

Parking his truck at an angle, facing the cabin, Zane left the headlights on so they could see the path to the stairs. He met Callie at her car.

"Need help with anything? Luggage?"

"I travel light. Been on the road for a while, so only one suitcase and my backpack." Callie opened the trunk to pull out the suitcase, but Zane beat her to it.

"Let me get that. Don't need you tripping on the stairs trying to carry that case. Once I get the lights on, it won't be so bad."

"I noticed on the way here the homes are elevated, including yours. Do you like stairs that much?"

"Keeps us in shape." Zane snickered. "Just kidding. We're not that far from the Gulf of Mexico and hurricanes bring floods. When you lose everything to flooding a couple of times, you either move or you take action."

"Why do you stay?"

"It's our home." Zane shrugged. Opening the door, he flicked a switch, and the room was bathed in light. "Speaking of home, this is mine."

"Yours? But…"

"It's not what you think." Zane didn't want her assuming the worst about him. "I don't live here. Cole and I live with Ridge in the big house we passed on the way in. I come in once a month or so to keep it clean, but otherwise, it stays empty."

"I'm sure there's a story, but I don't want to pry." Callie looked around, walking further into the room. "This is nice. I like the open floor plan. It's so spacious." She walked to the sliding glass door, peering into the darkness. "You have it all right here at your fingertips… a lovely home, the woods to roam in, and family close by."

Zane crossed the room to stand beside her. Her scent wrapped itself around him, and the urge to breathe her in was becoming overwhelming. To his disappointment, his wolf remained quiet.

25

"This is why I stay. Everything that means anything to me is right here."

"Not many can say that." Callie's voice was low.

"That's true enough. I don't take any of it for granted." Zane made himself step away. "Let me give you a quick tour, then I'll leave so you can get some rest. If you want coffee in the morning, come by the big house. We're all early risers, and there's always a pot on."

"Sounds good." Callie's mouth curved into a smile as she followed him.

"That door leads to the laundry room and back door." Zane gestured to a doorway at the back of the kitchen. "There are three bedrooms and a full bath. The main bedroom has an ensuite." He turned on the light in the largest bedroom. "There are towels and linens in the bathroom. Anything else you need, you can pick up at the store tomorrow."

"I appreciate you letting me stay here until I find a place of my own. How much do you want for rent while I'm here?"

"Don't worry about it. It's not like I'm using it." Zane raked his fingers through his short hair. "Get some rest. I'll see you in the morning." He turned to leave, then stopped and retraced his steps. Digging in his pocket, he pulled out a key. "Here's a key to the house. We're isolated out here, but I'd appreciate it if you'd keep the place locked.

"Of course." Callie reached for the key, slipping it into her jean's back pocket. "I'll take care of it like it was my own."

Zane turned away so Callie couldn't see the longing he knew was in his eyes. He had everything—except his Fated Mate. He was attracted to Callie, but so far, his wolf remained silent, not giving him a clue about the gorgeous female. He wanted a mate and a family. The desire welled up in him until he couldn't breathe. Zane needed to get outside, to run. His wolf was pushing at him hard.

Once outside, common sense prevailed. He couldn't leave his truck here and shift. If Callie saw his truck, she'd think he was creeping around. No, it was best to go home. Besides, he needed to talk to Ridge to see what he'd found out from Bishop. A run would have to wait.

"She get settled in all right?" Ridge asked as soon as Zane stepped through the door.

"Yeah, she's good." Zane dropped onto the couch and toed off his boots. "Heads up. I invited her for coffee in the morning. I don't have any food at my place, so she'll have to head to the store for supplies."

"Not a problem." Ridge gave him a searching look. "Has your wolf told you anything yet?"

"Not yet, but he's paying close attention when she's around. I'm kind of surprised he's being so cautious. It must be the *something else* I sensed about her that has us both hesitant." Zane met his brother's gaze. "Were you able to reach Bishop?"

"Yes. He met her at a bar she was working at in the Quarter years ago. They struck up a friendship and have kept in touch ever since. Whenever she lands in New Orleans, she gives him a call."

"So, we can trust her?"

"Seems so. I danced around the *something else* you'd mentioned. Bishop says she has a story, but it's hers to tell, so I didn't push."

"Good enough." Zane stood, picking up his boots. "Well, I'm going to hit the sack. Did you fill Cole in?"

"About Callie?" Ridge grinned. "Had to or he'd been all over that."

The low growl came from deep in Zane's chest.

Ridge laughed. "Go to bed, brother. Cole isn't going to mess with her until we know more."

Chapter 4

Callie wrapped the towel around her wet hair in a turban, then padded into the bedroom. Her suitcase stood against the wall where she'd left it a few hours ago. Too tired to bother with it, she'd stripped and slid between the sheets, wanting nothing more than sleep.

Rummaging through the case, she pulled out a pair of shorts and a crop top. She needed to go to the store to pick up some food and a few personal items. Hopefully, it would save her a trip to Bellerieve. First on her list, though, was that cup of coffee Zane had offered, which reminded her she needed to make sure there was a coffee maker here. She'd be surprised if there wasn't, considering this was Zane's home, and didn't that open up a bunch of questions.

Why leave this beautiful home standing empty to live with your brothers? Of course, family dynamics weren't quite her strong suit. She didn't have any siblings, and as for parents... Callie didn't dwell on what she couldn't change.

Tossing the towel into a basket in the bathroom, she ran a comb through her hair, freeing the tangles. Picking up the blow dryer, she hurriedly did her hair, quitting before it was fully dry. Opting for a messy bun, she grabbed her cell phone and headed for the kitchen, where she'd left her keys on the counter. Spotting the house key beside her own, she slipped the key onto a ring. Glancing at the appliances lined up neatly on the counter, she breathed a *yes* when she saw a coffee maker. One less thing she had to buy.

Locking the door behind her, she took in a deep breath as she surveyed the area. Oak, pine, and cedar trees, with the occasional dogwood, lined the bare ground serving as the road into the woods leading to the Landry's homes. Other than building the house, no changes had been made to the area. Zane hadn't infringed on nature, instead complementing his home to the forest around him. Serenity surrounded the home and Callie felt at peace for the first time in ages.

Starting up Jett, Callie let the engine warm up for a minute as she went through a mental list of things she needed to get today. Money wasn't an issue, but it didn't mean she could be careless. She'd gotten to where she was today by careful planning and living smart. That wasn't going to change.

The Hellcat rolled through the wooded lane at a slow rumble, coming to a stop before the two-story rustic dwelling. The house stood on bricked columns, leaving the bottom open to parked vehicles, boats, and four-wheelers.

A door slammed and Zane walked out to meet her, a welcoming smile on his handsome face.

"Who would have thought to find such a gorgeous home out here in the middle of nowhere," Calista breathed.

"Our mother always said living in the swamps didn't mean you had to live like swamp rats," Zane recalled with a fond smile.

Calista's brows furrowed, obviously confused.

"My mother was a bit more refined than Dad," Zane hurried to clarify. "She said if she had to live in the woods, she would live in comfort." He stretched his arms in front of the huge house. "Dad built her this."

"So, this is your family home?"

"Yeah, born and raised right here. After our parents died, we stayed here until Ridge met his mate. That's when Cole and I built homes of our own."

"Ridge has a mate?"

"No, not anymore." Sadness filled Zane's piercing blue eyes. "She died in a car accident a few years ago. Cole and I moved back in to be with Ridge. We weren't sure he would make it, so we stayed close." Zane shrugged. "Never saw a need to move back into my own place."

"I'm sorry for your losses." Callie wasn't sure what else to say.

"It's a part of life. We grieve and try to move on." Zane rubbed his hands together. "How about that coffee I promised?"

"That's why I'm here." Callie gave an impish grin. "I don't take offers of coffee lightly."

"Then I need to get you hooked up." He gestured toward the stairs. "This way to indulging your coffee gratification."

"Lead the way."

Callie noticed a similarity between this home and Zane's. Both had open floor plans and were furnished with comfort in mind. Every piece of furniture was sturdy and well-cared-for, and gleaming hardwood floors boasted of durability and timeless beauty.

Zane poured them each a mug of coffee and led her to the dining table. Creamer and sugar sat on a Lazy Susan in the middle of the table and Callie helped herself to both. She inhaled the rich fragrance before sipping the dark chicory.

"Now this is what I call coffee," she murmured in appreciation.

"Glad you like it. It's a local coffee, made in Baton Rouge."

"I've been on the road for so long I only know watered-down diner versions." Callie grimaced.

"You'll find out fast enough Cajuns appreciate their food and drinks, both rich and flavorful."

"Cajuns?"

"Most of the people in south Louisiana are Cajuns. Their ancestors were French immigrants who were expelled from Nova Scotia, eventually landing in Louisiana."

"You and your brothers are Cajun?"

"Yes, ma'am. Most everyone here is. You'll recognize them easily enough by last names, most are French."

"Does everyone speak French?"

"Very few do anymore. A few of the older ones speak it between themselves, but English has taken over, and Spanish is the secondary language now."

"Well, at least I won't have any language barriers to overcome." Callie wiped her brow.

"No, you're good on that front," Zane assured her with a wink.

"What time does the store open?" Callie glanced at her watch. "I need to get groceries for at least a week." She gave Zane a sidelong look. "By the way, how does the pay work?"

Zane pushed his chair back and walked over to the sideboard. Picking up an envelope, he placed it in front of Callie.

"You get paid every Friday, and bar tips are split between whoever is working the bar that night. This is your share from last night."

Callie opened the envelope, impressed with the amount of money.

"Thanks, this will help out a lot."

"To answer your first question, the store opens at eight and closes at the same time, Monday through Saturday. Everything shuts down on Sunday except the diner."

"I didn't notice the diner when I drove through."

"I'll have you know Bayou Crescent is a thriving community." He grinned to show he was teasing. "Not only do we have a garage and gas station, we also have a diner and a grocery store that's actually more of a general store. You can get almost anything from there... think of it as a backwoods Walmart, and of course, there's The Den. The Landry brothers take care of their own."

"You own all of them?"

"Well, the three of us do. We may be laid-back and country, but we're also entrepreneurs." Zane winked at her, and she couldn't help but smile. He was charming, in a rugged sort of way.

Callie covered the small distance to the kitchen and rinsed her cup, leaving it in the sink.

"Thanks for the coffee, but I need to get to your backwoods Walmart and stock up." She snapped her fingers as she remembered to ask, "What time do I need to be at The Den tonight?"

"Your shift begins at seven. Come a few minutes early so you can fill out the paperwork. It's standard employee stuff, but it will get Ridge off my case." Zane rolled his eyes. "He's a stickler for doing things by the book."

"Not a problem." Callie stifled a giggle at Zane's reaction. "Fifteen minutes enough, or should I be there earlier?"

"That should be fine."

"Guess I'll see you tonight." She needed to go, but there was a part of her that wanted to stay. She'd enjoyed her visit with Zane, not wanting it to end.

"Before you go..." He reached for her cell phone. "I'm putting my number in here. Call me if you need anything."

"Thanks, I will." She would probably never call unless there was a dire emergency, but liked that she had his number, and he had hers. She hadn't missed that he'd texted himself as soon as he'd put his number in her phone.

As Callie pulled onto the highway, she noticed what Zane had been talking about. The Den was situated farther back from the road, surrounded by huge oak trees, all dripping with Spanish moss. The gravel parking lot looked desolate without any trucks or bikes.

Next to it was a gas station/garage, the sounds of a pneumatic impact wrench filling the air as tires were changed. Bays and pumps were full as customers saw to their vehicle's needs.

An old-fashioned diner, appropriately named Road's End, was situated between the gas station and grocery store. A neon *Open* sign blinked in the window, and Callie noticed the parking lot was close to full, attesting to a decent breakfast menu. She made a mental note to check out the menu for days she didn't feel like cooking.

Pulling into the parking lot of the grocery store, she eased into a spot not far from the doors. Apparently, the population of Bayou Crescent were all early risers, going by the activity at the strip of businesses.

A blast of welcome cold air hit her as she entered. Grabbing a cart, she stood for a moment taking it all in. Zane hadn't been kidding. This store had everything—groceries, personal items, clothing, household items. It would take a couple of hours to peruse everything the place had to offer. Callie had hit the jackpot.

Chapter 5

The speedometer needle was closer to eighty than seventy-five, not that it mattered. Either way, he was still over the speed limit. Zane had spent way more time than he'd wanted in New Orleans going through a list of wholesalers for specific champagnes and whiskeys. It wasn't liquor they ordinarily kept on hand, but they were celebrating the mating of two pack members, and the parents of the mated couple had requested the preferred brands.

It was a small thing, one Zane usually didn't mind, but he'd had a gorgeous brunette on his mind all day and resented time away from her. He snorted. It wasn't like they'd had plans, but he could have come up with something. It was probably for the best. He didn't want her to think he was a creepy stalker, and he'd see her at work in a few more hours.

Ridge was waiting for him at the bar, and they swiftly unloaded his truck and stocked the bottles. They'd have time to put the champagne on ice when they came back later.

"Can I ask you something?" Zane opened two bottles of beer, handing one to Ridge.

"Sure, what's up?"

"When you first met Heather, what was your wolf's reaction to her?"

Ridge's eyes shuttered close.

Zane cursed himself for causing his brother pain, but he had no one else to ask. Ridge took a long pull on his beer, then began peeling the label from the bottle. Zane was beginning to think he wasn't getting an answer when his brother finally spoke.

"He was excited like a pup, wagging his tail and going around in circles. The whole time he was chanting *Mate, Mate, Mate.* There was no doubt. It didn't take me long to figure out he knew what he was talking about."

"I'm sorry to bring it up, but I needed to know."

"No need to apologize. I still miss her, guess I always will, but I'm learning to deal with it." Ridge's hazel eyes pierced Zane with a searching look. "What's going on with you and Callie? You asked for a reason."

"I'm confused, to be honest. When Callie is around, my wolf watches her closely, but he hasn't said anything to me yet."

"Has he ever done that with any other female?"

"Nope, not even a glimmer." Zane tossed his empty bottle in the trash. "Her scent overwhelms me whenever she's near, and we seem to have a connection, but I don't see it in her eyes. I'm wondering if I got it all wrong."

"You might be rushing it. She barely got here. Remember, I grew up with Heather, we knew we were mates when we were teens."

"You're probably right. I'm going to see if she'll spend the day with me tomorrow. I'll try to get to know her a little better. If she learns to trust me, she might be more willing to tell me about herself."

"Sounds like a plan." Ridge clapped Zane on the shoulder. "Let's head for home and grab something to eat before work. It's gonna be a long night."

A few hours later, pulling into the back parking lot of The Den, the first thing Zane noticed was Callie standing at the door with Kitty and Destiny. They were laughing and carrying on like best of friends, and it made Zane smile. It hadn't taken her long to win over the pack.

"Evening, ladies," Zane greeted the trio with what he hoped was a winning smile. "Y'all ready for a busy night?"

"Busier than last night?" Callie asked.

"I forgot to tell you." Kitty slapped her forehead. "Chad and Becky are newly mated and they're having the reception here. The drinks are all on a tab, and their parents will split it and pay at the end of the night."

"That goes for everyone who comes in the bar?"

"Yeah," Zane answered. "We were going to make it a private party, but Chad's parents wouldn't hear of it. They're more excited than the kids."

"There's going to be a ton of food, too," Destiny added excitedly. "We need to get in so we can set the tables up. The family will be here soon with the food and preparations."

Zane unlocked the door, pushing it open so Kitty and Destiny could enter. Before Callie went through, he caught her by the elbow.

"Before it gets crazy, I want to ask you something."

"Sure. What's on your mind?" Callie smiled up at him and he almost forgot the question.

"I was wondering if you'd like to take a little boat ride tomorrow."

"A boat? I don't think I've ever been on one."

"It's nothing fancy, but I want to show you around Bayou Crescent, and the best way is on the water."

"Sounds interesting. I'm always game for an adventure." She placed her hand on his arm. "What time? I'll set my alarm."

"I'll pick you up around ten." He walked her inside. "That okay with you?"

"Looking forward to it." Callie spotted Kitty and Destiny moving tables. "I better get to work. The girls might need my help."

Zane watched her walk away, admiring the sway of curvy hips, and the long hair cascading down her back. He focused on his wolf, who watched Callie with interest, but still remained silent. Shaking his head, Zane headed to the bar to set up. He had time to figure it all out.

Callie gave herself a mental shake. It wasn't like Zane asked her out on a date. He was simply being nice, offering to show her the area. If she planned on staying around, it was something she would need to know. She'd be lying though if the thought of spending the day with Zane Landry didn't give her a rush of excitement.

When she'd first walked into The Den and Zane looked at her with those piercing blue eyes framed by raven-black hair, her heart had skipped a beat or two. Callie had no business getting involved with anyone, but she couldn't help wanting to know more about the handsome shifter. What harm could there be in an innocent boat ride?

All too soon, thoughts of the sexy shifter were put on hold. People started streaming into the bar, some bearing trays of food, others with streamers and balloons. Within an hour, the rustic bar had been turned into a wedding reception any hall would have been proud of. Zane and Ridge filled the shelves with bottles of liquor, and kegs of beer were close at hand for convenience. Callie made sure every glass in the place was clean, and a stack of neatly folded towels lay on the shelf under the counter. They were as ready as they were going to get.

By nine o'clock the place was jumping. The band was a crowd-pleaser, playing popular dance tunes interspersed with slow songs. Watching the couples cling to each other during the slow numbers usually didn't bother her, but tonight it seemed to make her more aware of her loneliness. Taking a deep breath, she focused on filling glasses and plastering a forced smile on her face. There was no room in her life for romance or relationships. No one wanted someone who was broken.

"Why don't you take a break?" Zane nudged her arm, getting her attention. "Step outside and get some air. Ridge and I can handle this."

"Sounds like a good idea. Thanks." Callie tossed her towel onto the pile of dirty ones and gave Zane a grateful smile. "I won't be long."

"Take your time."

Humidity hit her like a wall as she stepped outside, but at least it didn't smell like a brewery. Walking to the corner, Callie leaned against the weathered side of the building and stared up at the stars. They shone brightly, far away from cities with lights and polluted air. She liked it here.

"What's a pretty thing like you doing out here all alone?"

Callie jerked her head toward the voice. She'd been so lost in her thoughts, she hadn't heard him approach. Narrowing her eyes, she stared at the man. He wasn't one of the regulars, and definitely wasn't one of the pack.

"I was taking a break, but it's time for me to get back inside." Callie stepped away from the building, but the man caught her by the arm.

"No need to rush away. They won't notice if you're gone for a few minutes." He backed her against the wall, a large hand cupping her face. "Stay here and keep me company. We can have our own private party."

Callie pushed against him, but he was a solid mass and didn't budge.

"Let me go. You'll only make matters worse if they come out looking for me."

He licked the side of her face and Callie shuddered.

"Ain't nobody gonna even notice you're gone."

When Callie heard the rasp of a zipper, she knew she had to do something. Pulling in her energy, amber light flared in her palms. Pushing against him this time, he flew across the parking lot, hit the grill of a truck, and slid to the ground with a thud. She heard the growl at the same time she saw the black wolf leap across the gravel and land in front of the fallen man.

"Callie! Are you all right?" Cole was at her side, concern etched on his face. "Zane was getting worried about you and when we opened the door, we saw you send that guy flying."

"I'm fine, just a little shaken." Callie pushed a lock of hair behind her ear and searched the area for the wolf. "Is the wolf Zane?"

A strangled cry for help and the snarl of a wolf caught their attention. Callie's eyes widened as she raced with Cole to get to Zane.

"Zane! Let him go," Cole yelled as he wrapped muscular arms around the wolf's chest, prying him off the screaming man. The wolf snapped at Cole, snarling his rage and fighting to get loose.

"You keep him away from me," the man screamed as he backpedaled away from them.

"Consider yourself lucky. Get off this property and don't come back," Cole warned.

The man scrambled to his car and jumped inside. Cole released Zane, watching his brother closely.

"Cole, look out!" Callie shouted.

The bullet report echoed loudly in the parking lot with no one else around. Cole dove for the ground, taking Callie with him. Zane lunged for the car, jumping onto the hood. More shots were fired, the windshield scored with cracks and starring. Zane dove off the hood, going for the driver's window, but the car was already in motion. Gravel and dust flew as the car fishtailed out the parking lot onto the highway.

Zane growled and started to go after the car, but stopped midstride, turning around and going to Callie's side. He whimpered as he nuzzled her side.

"I'm okay, Zane." She ran her hands through his thick, black fur looking for wounds. "Did you get shot?"

Zane chuffed and nudged against Callie.

"Let me get you inside and give Zane a minute to shift back."

"Okay." Callie looked back at Zane, who chuffed at her once again. "I'm going, I'm going," she grumbled.

Cole walked her to the bar, not leaving her until she went inside. Rushing to the counter, she faced Ridge.

"Everything all right, Callie?" Ridge asked, his voice low and gravelly.

"Yeah, it's all good." Giving him a shaky smile, she began filling pitchers of draft. Cole and Zane had seen her use her powers. That would bring up a lot of questions she'd rather not have to answer, but the Landry brothers had been nothing but kind to her. She owed them that much.

A few minutes later, Zane slipped behind the bar and filled orders like he'd never been gone. Other than a couple of sidelong glances at her, he said nothing about the incident outside. Callie wasn't foolish enough to think it would simply go away, but she'd settle for dealing with it later.

She kept a nervous eye trained on the door, but the man didn't return. A low voice in her ear assured her it wasn't going to happen.

"He's not coming back. You're safe."

Callie turned her head slightly to see Zane right behind her.

"I'm sorry, Zane. I didn't mean to cause any trouble."

Zane glanced around then captured her hand, pulling her off to the side.

"You have no reason to be sorry. None of it was your fault. If anything, it was mine. I should have told Cole to keep an eye on you."

"I don't need a babysitter, Zane. I can take care of myself."

"Obviously." The corner of his mouth quirked up the same time as his brow arched. "We need to talk, but I'll save it for later. Right now, I only want to make sure you're all right. That jerk crossed a line, and between Cole and me, he won't be back."

"I'm fine, and I do appreciate you and Cole looking out for me."

Zane cupped the side of her face and his thumb swept across her cheek. Callie's breath hitched at the gentleness of his touch.

"We... we need to get back to work," she stammered.

"Yeah, we'll talk tomorrow."

Chapter 6

Callie locked the door, closed her eyes, and tilted her head against the door. Thankfully, Zane nor Cole had questioned her about what they'd seen in the parking lot, but going by the questions in their eyes she wasn't off the hook, not by a longshot.

"Still looking for a wolf pack to accept you?"

Callie threw her hands in the air when she heard the voice in the shadowed corner of the living room.

"Of course, you would show up tonight." She flicked on the overhead lights. "What do you want, Rhistel?"

"What I've always wanted."

Tall and slender, with long, silver hair pulled back from a strong, arrogant face, the fae male stepped across the room to face Callie.

"Come with me to the Sidhe court. It's where you belong."

"The queen would kill me as soon as look at me. I'm a hybrid. There's no place for me with the Sidhe."

"It was the queen who sent me. Your powers are strong. You can serve Nephinae."

"I'm supposed to believe that?" Callie asked incredulously. "Nephinae killed my mother, and don't get me started on what she did to me."

Zane had left behind a well-stocked bar. Callie helped herself to a shot of whiskey in a tumbler, stared at it for a second, then added a second shot. She downed it in a gulp, grimacing at the burn.

"Come now, Calista, let bygones be bygones. It's all in the past. Put it behind you and move forward."

Callie stared at Rhistel as if he had grown two heads.

"This is not something you simply forget," she spat. "Besides, are you forgetting it was your sister the queen killed?

"No, I haven't forgotten." Rhistel winced. "It doesn't serve any purpose to speak of it around Nephinae. I'd rather not make waves at court." Rhistel's expression softened. "You have no place here. Your father kicked you out of his pack. The only place left is to come back with me. It's where you belong."

"I have no pack, thanks to Nephinae, and if you think that's a reason to go to the Sidhe court, you're sadly mistaken," Callie fumed, her fists clenching tightly at her sides.

"It's all the more reason to return," Rhistel cajoled.

He raised a hand to play with her hair and she slapped it away.

"Tell Nephinae if she wants me to hear her out, she has to undo what she did to me."

"You know she won't take the chance." Rhistel's voice dropped to a low murmur. "She did it to get you away from the shifters, to make you come back to your rightful home."

"And how well did that work?" Whereas Rhistel's voice had dropped, Callie's rose, along with her anger. "The Sidhe court has never been my home, and Nephinae is the one who made sure of it. She took away the one thing that made me whole. I won't have anything to do with her unless she fixes it."

"I'll give her your message." Rhistel shook his head, the beads in his braids clacking against each other. "Expect to see me again soon."

Callie didn't bother to see him out. He would leave the same way he got in—a drawn portal, the only way to reach the fae realm.

Collapsing on the sofa, Callie buried her face in her hands. Nephinae wasn't going to stop until she got what she wanted. The queen was relentless and vindictive enough to use any means at her disposal, though why she wanted Callie was a mystery, especially after all these years.

She needed to tell Zane what was going on, but she didn't know him well enough to know if she could trust him. Callie liked where she was—her job, the pack, and the Landry brothers. If they turned out to be like her father, she'd be out on the streets again, which would leave her vulnerable to the machinations of Queen Nephinae.

With a groan, Callie trudged to the bedroom and threw herself on the bed. She needed to get at least a few hours' sleep before Zane picked her up. Sending a quick prayer to whatever god was listening, she asked for the right words to tell Zane about herself.

Zane paced around the room, a tumbler of whiskey in his hand. There was no sense in trying to sleep. He was still seething that someone would dare attack Callie, or any female for that matter, on his property. The man had been a stranger, but he'd never forget his face or scent.

He also wondered about Callie. She'd been more than capable of handling the guy—had sent him flying across the parking lot, which was no little thing. His biggest question was *how* had she done it? When he'd stepped out of the bar, it was to see the man already in flight and Callie standing in front of the building, with her arms outstretched.

Zane had questions, but he needed to be careful how he went about getting answers. The last thing he wanted was to put Callie on the defensive or even worse, run from him. She hadn't done anything wrong, but she wasn't only a shifter, either. Zane wanted to know precisely what Callie Evans was.

"Grab a plate, Zane." The clatter of silverware on the table drew Zane's attention to his brothers in the kitchen. "The steaks are ready," Ridge announced as he sat at the table with a plate loaded with a huge slab of meat and baked potato.

"I want you to tell me what happened tonight in the parking lot."

"Cole didn't fill you in?" Zane glanced at Cole, who met his gaze openly as he placed a platter of steaks on the table.

"He did, but I want to hear your end of it. Did you talk to Callie about any of it yet?"

"No, she was a little shaken, so I told her we'd talk about it in the morning. I'm taking her around Bayou Crescent in my boat. Figured we'd have the day to sort it out, and I could get her to talk about herself and her powers."

"Good idea."

"As for the other," Zane said as he cut into his steak, "I told Callie to take a break. She'd been working nonstop since she'd walked through the door. After twenty minutes, I was getting a little worried, and mentioned it to Cole. We stepped outside and the first thing I saw was this guy flying across the parking lot. Callie was against the building with her hands outstretched. I didn't see how she did it, only the result—the guy landed past three rows of vehicles."

"I'll admit, I lost my shit. I shifted and jumped the guy. Wasn't planning on killing him, but I damn well wanted to get his attention. Next thing I knew, Cole and Callie were calling me off, the guy jumped in his car, then started firing off rounds at us. We're lucky he was a lousy shot."

"Cole said he didn't know the guy. What about you?" Ridge asked.

"Nope. Never saw him before, but his face and scent are burned in my brain. He'd be wise not to show up around here again," Zane declared.

"There was a lot of dust flying when he took off, but I saw his license plate. I'm going to call a friend at the sheriff's department and see if he'll run them. If I can get a name, we'll have something to work with," Cole added.

"Are we pressing charges?"

"Not yet," Ridge replied. "Pass it by Callie when you talk to her. If she wants to, we'll stand by her."

"Appreciate it."

"What could give her that kind of strength or power to toss a guy like she did?" Cole asked. "We all have enhanced strength but not to that level."

"Been wondering about it since I met her." Zane shrugged.

"She's done this before?" Cole's eyes widened incredulously.

"No, not the power thing, but I sensed something more than wolf. I simply haven't figured it out yet."

"It's also not something you come out and ask, either." Ridge pointed out. "It would be kinda rude."

"True," Cole agreed. "A witch, maybe? Definitely not a vampire."

"What else is out there?" Zane asked.

"Probably a bit of everything. We're not as well-versed in supernaturals as some, being isolated down here in bayou country." Ridge pushed away from the table and brought his empty plate to the sink. "I'm gonna call Maddox in the morning. Considering it was Bishop Callan who sent her down here, they're bound to know what types of Otherkind we have running around.

"The information could be helpful." Zane cleared his own dishes from the table and loaded the dishwasher. "I need to grab some sleep. Hopefully, Callie will be a little forthcoming about herself after what we witnessed tonight."

Chapter 7

Zane slapped at Cole's fingers when he snatched at a handful of catfish fillets on the platter next to the stove.

"Hands off!" Zane growled. "Those are for lunch for Callie and me."

"You and Callie, huh?" Cole smirked, licking his fingers clean. "You can't fry stuff at seven in the morning and not expect to find hungry wolves lurking about." Cole wiped his hands on a dishtowel, then crossed his arms across his chest as he watched Zane fry the rest of the fish. "Is the beautiful Callie aware my brother doesn't cook for just any female—especially fried catfish?"

"It's not a big deal. I thought I'd pack a lunch since we'll be out on the water for a few hours."

"It's a nice gesture, regardless." Apparently, Cole decided to play nice rather than keep up with relentless teasing. "Anything I can do to help?"

"Thanks, but I've got this. I'm packing everything separately for the cooler. This way she can dress her po'boy the way she wants, and we won't have soggy sandwiches."

Cole inspected the ice chest on the floor, half full of soft drinks, beer, and sandwich fixings.

"Looks like you're set." Cole ticked off on his fingers. "Got the extra gas cans filled? Phone charged? Checked the radio?"

"Ease up, li'l bro." Zane held up his hands in surrender. "I've been doing this since before you were born."

"Yeah, in your old age you might have forgotten something," Cole threw back.

"You did not just go there!"

"I think I did." Cole barked out a laugh and headed for the front door. "Have fun and don't do anything I wouldn't do."

"That leaves everything open!" Zane called after him. *Cheeky little bastard.* But Cole was Cole, and he was his little brother, which meant he usually got away with everything.

It didn't take long for Zane to clean up his mess in the kitchen. Leaving the packed cooler inside, he headed outside to stow the rest of his gear in the truck. His sixteen-foot aluminum hull boat was parked at his house and wouldn't take but a few minutes to uncover and hook up to his truck.

It had been a while since Zane had been out on the water and he was looking forward to the excursion. If Callie proved to be a 'water baby' it would be icing on the cake. There wasn't a single family in the settlement who didn't reap benefits from living so close to the water. Diets were supplemented with fish and other seafood delicacies from the local waterways and open gulf. Thanks to extended summer weather, many weekends and holidays were spent water-skiing, fishing, or hanging out on party barges. The pack even claimed a private island for their full moon runs, but you had to get there by boat, making it secluded from outsiders.

Glancing at his watch, Zane still had time to kill but was getting antsy. He wanted to be out on the water and wanted Callie with him. Hopefully, the day would go well. With a shrug, he headed to the house, grabbed the ice chest, and loaded it in the back of the truck. He wouldn't rush Callie if she wasn't ready. He'd take his time hooking up the boat and packing what they would need for the day.

Easing the Raptor around to the side of the house, Zane backed up to the small boat under the concreted carport. Landscaping, large rocks, and shrubbery concealed the open foundation from the front and back, leaving only the sides open to access.

Pulling the cover from the aluminum hull boat, Zane smiled in satisfaction when he saw the cover had done its job. No accumulation of water or critters awaited him. Within minutes, the cover was stashed in a nearby tote, and the boat was hooked up to the truck. Zane was loading the last of the gear when he heard Callie coming down the steps.

"You're early," Callie called out, a wide smile lighting up her face.

"I am, but there's no rush. I needed to check out the boat and load it. Figured I could do it while you finished getting ready."

"All I have to do is grab my keys and lock the door behind me." Callie waved a hand down her curvy frame. "Is this okay?"

Zane took in the bikini top, cutoff shorts, and sneakers. A denim shirt with rolled sleeves, tied off at the waist, would give her protection from the scorching sun. Her long, glossy hair was pulled up into a messy bun. He swallowed hard. She was a vision even in the most casual attire.

"It's perfect." Zane had to force his gaze back to her eyes, which were glinting with amusement. "You sure you've never been on a boat?"

"Nope. New experience for me, but I did check with Destiny and Kitty about what I should wear." She laughed now that her secret was out. "I didn't want to look inexperienced."

"You look like you've spent your life on the water." Zane grinned.

"I've spent a fair amount of time on beaches and in the water." Callie seemed to think about her answer. "But I never had the opportunity to go boating. You'll be my first."

"Your first, huh?" Zane knew his eyes had flashed color, and Callie had seen it, going by the cheeky smirk.

"Yep, so you better make it special."

"I'll try my best." Zane's voice was husky as he double-checked the hitch and safety chain. "Why don't you grab what you need and lock up? We can head out anytime."

"Won't be but a sec."

Zane watched her sprint up the stairs, admiring her long, tan legs as they climbed. He growled low as he adjusted his jeans, visions of her legs wrapped around him. This would be a torturous day if he didn't get a handle on his libido.

Good to her word, Callie was back in a flash. Opening the passenger door, he gestured to her.

"Climb in, milady. Your chariot awaits."

She giggled, and Zane swore he'd never heard anything sweeter. Closing the door and crossing around to the driver's side, he focused on his wolf. Sure enough, he was there, sitting quietly and watching.

What was going on?

As far as he knew, this wasn't how it worked. Callie was his Fated Mate, or she wasn't. His beast wasn't giving him a clue, which left Zane confused and more than a little frustrated. With a huff of exasperation, Zane swung into the driver's seat and started up the truck.

"Is everything okay?" Callie's forehead creased in concern.

Zane swore to himself, reaching over to pat her hand in reassurance.

"Nothing for you to worry about." He flashed her a smile. "I thought of something I need to take care of, but I can do it later." He hoped she wouldn't sense the white lie. Most shifters could tell when someone was lying, but they had to be paying close attention.

"If you're sure..." Her expression clearly showed her doubt. "We can always do this another time."

"No, ma'am. This is our day, and nothing is going to get in our way."

Callie seemed to take his words at face value and relaxed back in the seat.

"I'm glad. I have to say I'm looking forward to this. I've heard a lot of talk about the bayous and swamps when I was in New Orleans, but this is the real deal." She turned in her seat to face him. "Any chance I'll get to see an alligator?"

Zane couldn't help it, he laughed out loud.

"If you see only one, I'm doing something wrong."

Callie's eyes widened.

"The swamps are their home, so there are plenty of gators out there, but don't worry. You're perfectly safe with me. They won't bother us."

"So, they're not as dangerous as they're played up to be?"

"Don't kid yourself. Gators are lethal, and they're fast, but they're used to the amount of boat traffic around here and we make it a point not to feed them."

"You *feed* them?" Callie's expression turned horrified.

"*We* don't." Zane sniggered. "But a lot of people who run swamp tours do. It's a big hit with the tourists."

"Sounds a lot like throwing chum to the sharks."

"Same principle, except we don't want to start a feeding frenzy. That would be disastrous."

"Are you sure this little excursion of yours is safe?" Callie rubbed her arms briskly.

"We'll be fine, I promise."

Zane winked at her as he slowed the truck and made a semi-circle, then backed down a ramp into the water. Throwing the vehicle into park, he jumped out and headed toward the boat. Callie followed to watch. With years of practice, it took only minutes to unhook the boat and push it into the slip, then tie it off to a mooring while he parked the truck.

Zane swallowed hard as he crossed the small parking lot to reach Callie and the boat. She was standing on the pier, staring out over the water. He couldn't remember the last time a woman had affected him like this. It was more than her looks, though she was a true beauty. There was something special about her that drew him like a moth to a flame.

"Ready?" Zane grinned at Callie and hopped into the boat, extending a hand to her.

"I guess I'm committed now." Taking his hand, she nimbly leapt into the boat. Zane steadied her with his free hand as she landed.

"Have a seat, and I'll get this party started." Zane laughed lightly as he untied the boat from the mooring and pushed off. Starting the engine, he eased the aluminum hull deeper into the bayou.

They rode in silence for a few minutes, Zane checking the waters for anything that could snag on the propeller, and Callie sitting quietly, watching the swamp unfold before her. He sensed her before he felt her beside him.

"It has its own kind of beauty, doesn't it?" Callie asked in a low voice.

"The bayou? Yeah, it's not for everyone, but it's all I've ever known."

"Have you ever wanted to live anywhere else?" Callie was watching him now instead of the scenery.

"Can't say I ever thought about it." Zane shrugged. "You know how packs are, the proverbial homebody. We tend to stay put."

"What about travel?" Callie persisted. "Surely, there are places you've wanted to see."

"I traveled a bit, when I was younger." Zane wasn't sure where or what her questions were leading to, but they were making him think carefully about his answers. "I've seen some fascinating things and met interesting people, but I always came home. This is my place. I'm needed here."

"What about you?" Zane decided it was time for Callie to answer a few questions. "You've obviously traveled. Your wolf doesn't mind you being away from your pack?"

He hadn't meant to throw it out there so bluntly, but shifters, especially wolves, were pack. Lone wolves didn't seek out packs, and he'd never heard of a female going lone wolf or rogue.

Callie turned her head, but not before Zane saw the flinch and glisten of unshed tears. He cursed under his breath and throttled the boat down to a stop.

"Damn, Callie, I'm sorry. I didn't mean to say anything that would hurt your feelings. It came out all wrong."

She waved his apology away, then brushed away a tear.

"Don't apologize. You have every right to ask. Pack safety is a priority, and I'm an unknown, even with Bishop's sanction." Callie took a deep breath and faced him. "When my mom... died, my father took her loss badly. He had little patience with me, letting the mated females of the pack raise me. By the time I was a teen, he couldn't stand the sight of me."

Zane reached for Callie's hand and urged her to sit on the small bench seat. Starting the engine, he eased the boat down the bayou.

"What happened then?" Zane asked, encouraging her to continue her story.

"He'd been drinking a lot and stumbled into my room one night."

Tears trickled down Callie's cheeks, and Zane prayed she wasn't going to tell him what he was thinking. He would have to find the man and kill him.

"He told me I had to leave. I couldn't stay with the pack anymore. I reminded him too much of my mother, but I didn't have her powers, so I was of no use to him." Callie glanced up at him with a shaky smile. "I packed a small bag and left... haven't been back since."

Zane had made his way to the island while Callie told her story. Tying the boat off to a mooring, he knelt before her.

"How old were you?"

"Sixteen."

"Son of a... you were no more than a child!" Zane bit out.

"I grew up fast. I had to if I wanted to survive."

"Where did you go?"

"The nearest town for a while. I managed to get odd jobs, living in shelters and abandoned buildings. After that, I took the next bus going to a big city. By then, I was eighteen and able to land better jobs. I rented a room and saved up enough money for a car. It was a clunker, but she got me to the next town." Callie shrugged. "It's been my life ever since. I stay on the move because shifters

67

are territorial, and I didn't want to make any waves."

Zane couldn't argue about shifters being territorial. No matter what animal they were, they were alike on that score and didn't welcome lone shifters into their boundaries.

"What about your mom's family? Wasn't there anyone you could've turned to?" Zane had a feeling he knew the answer, but he needed to ask. The only way he would find out about her powers was to get her to talk about her mother.

"Not really." Callie's response was hesitant. "I have an uncle, but he's not in a position to help me." She fidgeted with a stray curl of chestnut hair. "It's complicated."

"I can tell you don't want to talk about it, and ordinarily, I wouldn't push the matter, but I need to know more about your powers, Callie. My duty is always to the pack, and I need to know you're not a threat."

"I get it." Callie rubbed the bridge of her nose. "I truly do, but there are some things that you're better off not knowing."

Zane could see the fear in her eyes as she went on.

"If I must leave, I'll understand, but I'm asking you to take a chance on me. I would never hurt anyone in the pack. I'm not like that. But I... I need to be under a pack's protection. I'm tired of being alone and always on the move."

Zane stared off into the distance, his mind racing. What she was asking for was impossible. Ridge would offer her sanctuary, but he would want to know why she needed it.

"No alpha will grant sanctuary without knowing more about your powers."

"I was afraid of that," Callie said in a low voice.

"Give me something, Callie." Zane reached for her hand, squeezing it gently in his much larger one. "I want to help you, but my hands are tied unless you work with me."

"My mother's people aren't from around here, and they tend to keep to themselves. They all wield magic of some kind. The ones with purer bloodlines are stronger and have more powers. My mother was one of them."

"You mentioned you don't have your mother's powers. What could she do?"

"She was able to read minds and mentally persuade others to do her bidding. My father took advantage of it often. When mine started developing, they weren't of any use to him. What he didn't know, and I didn't bother to tell him, was as we grow older, the purer lines develop more skills, gaining strength and power.

"Thank you." Zane smiled tenderly at her. "I'll talk to Ridge when we get back. I'm sure we can

69

work something out." He stood, pulling her along with him. "In the meantime, I want to show you our island. I brought lunch and figured we could eat out here."

Chapter 8

Callie grabbed a blanket and helped Zane carry the cooler to a clearing shaded by huge oak trees. Spreading the blanket on the ground, Zane pulled out container after container.

"What exactly do you have in there?"

"Everything you need to make a catfish po'boy," Zane answered with a grin. "Ever had one?"

"Yes and no." Callie gave a half-shrug. "I've had po'boys, but never one with catfish."

"Then you're in for a treat. I fried the fish myself this morning."

She watched Zane dress his sandwich, then started preparing her own.

"Coke or beer?"

"A beer sounds good."

The temperature had risen as the morning wore on, and Callie was glad she'd opted for shorts. It had to be ninety degrees already, and she could feel a trickle of sweat running down her back.

"My kind of woman." Zane unscrewed the cap and passed her a bottle, taking a long pull on his own. "Nothing better on a hot day."

Callie took a bite of her sandwich, her eyes widening in pleasure as the mixture of flavors hit her taste buds.

"This is so good."

"Glad you like it." Zane's smile broadened at her praise.

Surrounded by the sounds of nature, Callie listened to the occasional splash of water and croak of frogs. What she didn't recognize, Zane pointed out to her. The flap of wings was an egret taking off after filling its belly, and the odd chirping was crickets. She knew Zane had grown up here, but she hadn't realized how attuned he was to the land around him. He let out a low groan, pulling Callie from her thoughts.

"I don't know if I want to take a run or a nap," Zane chuckled, patting his nonexistent belly.

Callie froze, swallowing hard.

"How about it?" Zane looked at her expectantly. "Want to go for a run? We've got the whole island to ourselves. This is where we have our full moon runs."

"I... I can't," Callie stammered. She felt heat rush up her neck and spread across her cheeks. Hanging her head, she mumbled, "I'm sorry, Zane."

He reached over and raised her head with a gentle finger under her chin, confusion stamped on his handsome features.

"What do you mean, you can't? Callie, talk to me."

Tears brimmed over and trickled down her cheeks as she hugged herself, rocking back and forth. When Zane tried to move closer, she put up a hand to stop him.

"Don't, Zane." She hiccupped and sniffed, trying not to bawl like a baby. "I knew better, but I hoped it would be different this time."

"What do you mean?" Zane persisted. "Let me help you."

"You can't. No one can." At last, she managed to meet his gaze. "I'm broken. I can't shift."

"How is that even possible?"

Callie rose to her feet, wiping the tears from her face.

"The leader of my mother's people wanted me to live with them after my mom died. I refused, and she bound my wolf. She thought if I couldn't shift, I'd have no choice but to return."

"But you didn't..."

"No, I didn't... I couldn't." Callie bit her bottom lip, thinking furiously. She had to make a decision—tell Zane the truth... all of it or leave now. "She was responsible for my mother's death. There was no way I could go there and look at that monster every day. Better to deal with my broken wolf and go it alone."

"Callie..."

"I'm half-fae, Zane."

Callie turned away, staring out over the water, and waited. Fae were not friends with shifters. There was no trust or love lost between the two. In fact, many packs considered consorting with the fae forbidden. Her own mother had been killed because of that way of thinking.

Strong hands clasped her shoulders and turned her around. Before Callie could react, she was pulled into Zane's warm embrace. She leaned into him as his arms tightened possessively around her. He nuzzled her neck, his mouth moving down her throat until their lips met in a warm and tender kiss.

"You're not alone anymore," he told her, his voice thick with emotion. "I don't care that you're fae either. Give me a chance, Callie. Give *us* a chance."

"Us?"

"Yes, us. Don't you feel it?"

Callie felt her heart stutter at Zane's tender smile.

"My... my wolf..." she started.

"I know. My wolf has been watching you but hasn't given me any inclination whether you're my mate or not. I know why now... he can't sense *your* wolf." Zane kissed her again, his lips crushing against hers, his body heat seeping into her skin. "You're mine, Callie. I know you are."

"But what if we aren't mates, Zane?"

"But what if we are?"

"I'm not sure. This is going too fast." Callie broke free from his embrace. "I don't want you to get hurt." In a small voice she breathed, "I don't want to get hurt, either."

"I get that, I do," Zane said. "I'm not rushing anything, but I don't want you to leave."

Callie packed away what was left of their lunch, more to keep her hands busy than anything else.

"What if Ridge won't let me stay? I won't have a choice then."

"He will." Zane saw her doubtful expression and pushed the cooler out of the way, grabbing both her hands in his. "Ridge is reasonable and fair. He knows I'm attracted to you... There's no way he'd send you away if there's any chance you're my Fated Mate." Zane leaned closer and kissed her lightly. "Trust me."

"I do trust you." Callie smiled despite her misgivings.

"But I don't want to get your hopes up..."

"Not another word on the subject. I'll talk to Ridge this evening, and everything will work out." Zane rose, pulling Callie up with him. "I promised you a tour and gators. We're wasting sunlight."

He grinned at her, and Callie couldn't help but smile back. He was so charming, persuasive, and so damn sexy. She sighed inwardly. Her heart didn't stand a chance against Zane Landry.

True to his word, Zane's tour included Bayou Crescent, the pack's private island, and the swamps, which were a world apart from anything she'd ever seen before. There was a raw and primal beauty about it—huge cypress trees with Spanish moss hanging from branches, long-legged egrets which should have been gangly but were actually quite graceful in their movements, and turtles perched on logs and rocks, peacefully slumbering in the sun.

Zane idled the engine, coming to a stop. Callie looked at him curiously.

"I thought you were going to show me the alligators."

"Look over there." Zane pointed toward the bank a little ahead of them.

Callie's gaze followed the direction he was pointing to. She shaded her eyes with a hand and squinted.

"I don't see anything except a few logs in the water."

Zane's laugh was low, deep, and all too alluring. Callie suppressed a groan at the sheer sexiness of the sound.

He picked up a small branch floating by the boat and threw it toward the logs. The water stirred and one of the 'logs' opened its gaping maw, showing way too many teeth for Callie's comfort. Their slumber interrupted, two or three started to thrash around, their tails flailing in the air.

"Ohh! They're huge!" Callie exclaimed.

"Yeah, those are a good size, probably nine or ten feet each."

"Are we safe? Shouldn't we move on or something?" Callie watched the gators, nervous yet fascinated by the reptiles.

"We should be okay, as long as we don't antagonize them." Zane winked at her. "I think that's enough for one day. It's about time to head back in."

Callie couldn't help but be a little relieved. The idea of seeing alligators in their natural habitat had been exciting at first. Seeing them this close made her realize exactly how dangerous they actually were.

"Sounds like a plan to me," Callie conceded gratefully. "I appreciate you taking the time to show me all this. I really enjoyed the tour."

"It was my pleasure." Zane beamed at her. "If you want, we can take the boat out another time and go fishing or just cruise around."

"I might take you up on it," Callie said. "This is all new to me, so I'm open to an adventure."

Zane bore down on the throttle, easing away from the gators, and heading to clear waters. He pointed out landmarks, telling stories about each one.

Callie soaked it in, trying to remember all the details but in the end, she simply enjoyed time spent with Zane. He knew the land like the back of his hand and was proud of his home and heritage. She envied it because it was something she would never have.

All too soon they were back at the landing, and Zane was loading the boat onto the trailer. Callie admired the grace and ease Zane displayed, not to mention the flexing of toned muscles as he went about the process. She felt rather useless, standing around watching him, but vowed to pitch in next time.

Zane opened the passenger door for Callie, giving her a hand up into the cab even though she could have easily hopped up with no assistance. She appreciated the gesture.

As Zane's home came into view, they exchanged a glance, full of unspoken words. At last, he broke the silence.

"I'll talk to Ridge and let you know what he says."

"If you don't mind, I'd rather hear it firsthand," Callie said. "I'll know more from his expression than his words."

"You sure?"

Zane's sidelong glance was full of concern, and it touched Callie's heart.

"Yeah, I'd rather deal with this head-on." Callie tried to smile, but it was a halfhearted attempt. "The wait would only drive me crazy."

"Well, let's do this. Cole's inside, too. Might as well make it official."

Zane put the truck in park and skirted around the front of the vehicle, opening the door for her. When he extended his hand, Callie took it, her chest tightening with apprehension of what was to come.

The realization hit her hard. In the few days she'd been at Bayou Crescent, she'd grown attached to the small community and the pack who resided there. Callie didn't want to have to leave. She especially didn't want to have to leave Zane. He'd already claimed her heart.

Chapter 9

Callie was a nervous wreck by the time she reached the top of the stairs with Zane. He gave her an encouraging smile and squeezed her hand. She appreciated the gesture, but it did nothing to alleviate her fear.

Holding the front door open for her, Zane gestured toward the couch. Cole was sitting in a recliner, playing a video game, and Ridge claimed the other chair, his nose buried in a book. It appeared to be a peaceful Sunday... one she was getting ready to disrupt.

"Y'all are back early," Cole said with an easy grin, turning off the game and dropping the game controller on the floor.

"Everything all right?" Ridge marked his place and set the book on the table between him and Cole.

"Guess that depends on your decision." Zane sat next to Callie, still holding her hand. "Callie told me a little about her family, and as Alpha, it's something you need to know." He turned to Callie. "We can't help you if we don't know all the details. Remember, we're on your side."

Zane brought her hand to his lips and kissed her fingertips, then released his hold. He sat back, giving Callie space to gather her thoughts and tell her story.

Callie nervously fidgeted with the hem of her shirt. She'd buttoned it when they'd come inside. The bikini top had been fine out on the boat, but here, under the watchful eyes of Zane's brothers, she felt vulnerable and exposed.

"I guess it's for the best if I start at the beginning," Callie said with a nervous smile. "My father is Alpha of the Timbercreek Wolves in Cheyenne, Wyoming. My mother wasn't his Fated Mate, marrying him instead for security and the protection his position gave her. She was fae, a member of the royal court." Callie held her breath when Ridge's brow rose and Cole sat a little straighter, but neither male said a word. Clearing her throat, Callie continued.

"I explained earlier to Zane that all fae wield magic of some kind. Those with pure bloodlines are stronger, having more powers. As one of the royal court, my mother had one of the purest bloodlines. She could read minds and mentally persuade others to do her bidding. It was because of that power my father married her."

"When Nephinae, queen of the fae, discovered my mother had given birth to a hybrid, she ordered my mother to return to court. My mother refused. I was only five when assassins murdered her."

"I'm sorry for your loss," Ridge offered. "Did your father retaliate?"

"The fae live on another realm." Callie shrugged. "Without a way to track them, my father didn't bother. He was enraged when my mother died but it wasn't until much later that I understood it had nothing to do with his love for her, but the loss of her power."

Zane went to the kitchen, returning with a cold bottle of water. Callie gave him a grateful smile when he handed it to her. Parched from talking, she downed the bottle hastily.

"My father had no interest in me, giving me to the mated females to raise. Not long after my powers started developing, the queen appeared when I was alone in the forest. She wanted me to return to court with her."

Callie closed her eyes as the memory of that day washed over her, still as fresh as the day it happened.

"There was no way I could live with the person who was responsible for my mother's death. I refused, waiting for the same fate as my mom. Instead, the queen bound my wolf. She told me if I couldn't shift, I would have no choice but to go to the fae realm. Nephinae told me to call on her when I changed my mind."

Callie raised sorrow-filled eyes to Ridge. She didn't want his pity, but she did want his help.

"I didn't know how to tell my father I was broken. It turned out I didn't have to worry. He'd been drinking heavily all day and later that night, he told me I had to leave. I couldn't stay with the pack anymore. I reminded him too much of my mother, but I didn't have her powers, so I was of no use to him. I was sixteen. I've been on my own ever since."

"What about the fae, Callie? Eventually, the queen will come searching for you again. What happens then?"

Callie stared at the floor, hot tears welling in her eyes. She'd told the Landry brothers this much, she would have to tell them the rest, though it would mean she would have to move on... again.

"My uncle, Rhistel, came to me the other night. The queen wants me in her service. I told him I wouldn't even speak to her unless she frees my wolf."

"What if she does?" Ridge's voice was soft and low, but Callie wasn't lulled by the tone. His words were as sharp as a sword's blade, which was sheathed for the moment.

"She won't. She would never give me back my full power."

"This has the sound of a war brewing," Cole said, narrowing his gaze at Callie.

Zane's growl came from deep in his chest as he sat closer to Callie, draping an arm around her shoulder.

"Control your wolf, brother. Callie is in no danger from us," Ridge reprimanded. The elder brother warned Cole with a glance. "Isn't that right?"

"I wasn't threatening her," Cole insisted. "Simply stating a fact—one we need to take into consideration."

"Cole has a valid point," Ridge agreed as he stared pointedly at Callie. "My first priority is to the safety of the pack—always."

Callie felt the burn of tears threatening again but managed to blink them back.

"I understand, Alpha. I'll pack and leave immediately."

She felt Zane tense beside her and saw the shared glance between Cole and Ridge but didn't understand what it meant.

"Hold on there." Ridge smiled, holding his hands up. "I didn't say you had to leave." He denied resignedly. "I'm fairly sure if you left, I'd lose a brother in the bargain."

Callie's eyes widened at his words and turned to Zane, who didn't say a word, but the expression on his face told her Ridge knew his brother all too well. The Landry brothers were a tightknit unit, and the last thing she wanted was to come between them.

"No, I don't want to start any trouble with anyone, especially the three of you."

"It's not going to come to that," Ridge told her with a wink. "I do have a few more questions, if you don't mind."

"Of course, anything."

"You told us about the queen visiting you in the woods, and your uncle the other night. Have you been approached by any other of the fae?"

Callie thought back over the years she'd been on her own. She was twenty-six, so there were ten years to cover. She rubbed her forehead as she rewound the years in her mind. She was more than a little surprised to realize how few interactions she'd actually had with the fae.

"Rhistel visits me from time to time. He's the only link I have to my mother, and I think we both cling to that. He was very close to her and was upset when she married my father. As far as the others, they may have been watching me, but I'm unaware of it. I figured since I'm unable to shift, the queen deems me harmless."

"But she wants you now," Cole interjected.

"True, but I refused her offer. Rhistel said he would return soon with the queen's reply."

"Before we jump the gun, how about we wait and see what Callie's uncle comes back with?" Ridge turned to Callie. "Do you think your uncle would harm you in any way? Would he come with reinforcements to make you return?"

Callie bit her lip in agitation. The thought of being forced to return to the Sidhe court had never entered her mind. Would the queen actually go that far?

"I don't believe Rhistel would ever harm me, but then again, he won't blatantly disobey the queen." Callie forced herself to meet Ridge's gaze. "I wouldn't put anything past Nephinae. She's altogether capable of getting what she wants. I hardly thought I'd be on her radar, though. I'm not that important."

Ridge sat back, long legs stretched out as he thought. Zane gave her an encouraging hug, which she found more than comforting. A sidelong glance at the third brother found him sitting quietly, totally expressionless. Callie bet Cole was one hell of a poker player.

She wanted to pace the floor, at least move around, but didn't dare. Callie had answered all their questions and told them all she knew. There was nothing left but wait for Ridge's decision.

"Callie, if I offer you sanctuary, can I count on you to be forthcoming with any information this uncle of yours tells you?"

"Yes, of course. I owe no loyalty to the Sidhe court or my father's pack." Callie's nails dug into her palms. *Was she being foolish to get her hopes up?*

Ridge sat up, rubbing his palms together.

"I don't want to say too much just yet. I need to make a phone call, but if I'm right, there may be a way to help you with your wolf."

Callie's eyes widened in surprise.

"Don't hold me to that. I said there *may* be a way. We'll try to protect you the best we can, but I don't know much about the fae. That's another phone call."

"I'm sorry I can't help you. I was too young when my mother died, and Rhistel hasn't told me a lot about the Sidhe court."

"We'll get around it," Ridge assured her. "You said your uncle visited you the other night, how did he find you?"

"Our family bloodline is an automatic link. He opens a portal and finds me wherever I am."

"There's no way to protect you from that..."

"There's the last resort," Zane offered.

"There is that," Ridge agreed. "But let's leave it for the moment. How about you stay with Callie for the time being?" Ridge met Callie's gaze. "Is there a problem with my brother staying with you?"

"No, not at all. It's his house, after all," Callie said in a rush. *The only problem will be keeping my hands off him.*

"Good enough. I know it won't be a hardship on him." Ridge smirked. "Cole will set up a team to patrol your house. We'll protect you the best we can. Keep in mind, we're shifters and have no magic to fight the fae with. That's why I need to know what's going on at all times."

"I promise, Alpha. Thank you so much for taking a chance on me. I'll do my best to see you don't regret it."

"Thank you, Ridge," Zane said, his voice husky with emotion.

"If there's any chance at all she's your Fated Mate, she's worth fighting for, brother."

Chapter 10

Zane felt the tension release from his shoulders hearing Ridge's decision. He wasn't kidding himself, and Cole was probably right. There would be trouble, if not a war of some kind, but he would deal with things as they came. The most important thing was Callie was staying. He wouldn't dwell on what would or wouldn't come of it. He would savor the moments he had with her now.

He grabbed Callie's hand and pulled her up beside him.

"Come with me. I need to throw a few things in a bag. I'll come back later for more." She gave him a nervous smile but went willingly enough.

Entering the bedroom, Zane closed the door behind them and pulled Callie into his arms. He gazed into her brown eyes, losing himself in their dark depths. Lowering his mouth over hers, he kissed her slowly and tenderly, making himself wait until she gave herself to the kiss and to him. When she breathed a small moan, his arms tightened around her.

Zane searched for his wolf, finding him immediately. He was lying with his muzzle resting on his paws. The beast kept silent but was content. It had to mean something.

Ending the kiss as unhurriedly as he'd started it, he pulled away from Callie's tempting lips and soft curves.

"I needed to make sure you wanted this," Zane husked into her ear.

"You could have simply asked." Callie gave a knowing smile, palming his cheek.

"Wouldn't have been near as fun."

"True, and I'm certainly not complaining." Callie stepped back and surveyed the room. "Is there anything I can do to help you pack?"

"Nah, won't be but a sec." Zane's voice was muffled from the walk-in closet. A duffel bag landed on the floor with a thump, and Zane closed the doors. Grabbing the bag, he set it on the foot of the bed and opened a dresser. He threw socks, underwear, and t-shirts into the duffel with precision.

"A boxer man, are you?" Callie giggled as she watched him pack.

"A man's gotta breathe," Zane teased back with a wink. He crossed into the ensuite, threw a few things into a shaving kit and waved it at Callie. "This ought to do it for a few days."

"It's not like you have to go a great distance if you forgot anything."

"I'm a man who likes to be prepared... and if you say one word about a Boy Scout, I'll put you over my knee," Zane said with a warning finger.

"Really, now?" Callie laughed. "You may have opened yourself up to a barrage of scout jokes."

Zane growled, but Callie laughed again, and he joined her. Callie was his type of woman, in every kind of way. He only wished his wolf would get on board already.

Zane pulled up to his house and backed the boat into its spot. He would have to rinse it off before covering it, but it could wait a few minutes. He wanted to get settled in with Callie first.

"If you grab the bag Ridge gave us, I'll unload the cooler," Zane said. "Leave a couple of those steaks out, and I'll grill those for dinner."

"Sounds great. I'm sure I have some potatoes I can bake. I still have time to run to the store if we need anything."

"Give me a few minutes, and I'll go with you."

"Zane, is it going to be like this from now on?" Callie's smile disappeared. "I don't want you, or anyone else, to be burdened with following me around."

He set the cooler down and walked over to stand in front of Callie. Taking the bag from her, he pulled her into an embrace.

"You are not a burden, especially not to me. I'll go with you because I want to protect you, and I don't want anything to happen to you."

"I've always been on my own. It's hard for me to accept help."

"You're not on your own anymore." Zane wiped a tear from Callie's cheek with the pad of his thumb. "At least, not as long as you want to stay in Bayou Crescent... and with me."

"I'm beginning to think that sounds pretty good."

Callie smiled up at him, taking Zane's breath away. *Where had this beauty been all his life?*

"Come on, let's get my gear in the house. I'll tend to the boat, then we can run up to the store.

Make a list of what you think we'll need, or I'll buy out the place." Zane laughed. "I never remember everything and end up picking up stuff I don't need."

"I think everyone is guilty of that." Callie grinned.

Together, they got everything upstairs, and Zane felt awkward for the first time in ages.

"I'll grab a spare bedroom."

"I can't let you do that," Callie exclaimed. "Give me ten minutes and I'll clear my stuff out of your room."

"No, Callie. The arrangement was for you to stay here. I want you to stay in this bedroom. The spare is fine for me."

"I appreciate the gesture, Zane, but this is your home."

He could see Callie was seriously distressed about the situation, and he couldn't let that happen.

"You're right, it's my home, so I call the shots, and you get the main bedroom." He laughed when Callie rolled her eyes. Pulling her into his arms, he kissed her lightly. "Besides, who knows? We might end up sharing the room before it's all said and done."

"You're that sure of yourself?"

"Nah, but I'm hopeful."

"What am I going to do with you?" Callie buried her head in his chest, her shoulders shaking from muffled laughter.

"Don't leave that hanging because I've got a multitude of answers." Zane nuzzled her ear, then lightly nipped her earlobe.

Callie gasped, fisting his shirt.

"Why do I have the feeling I won't have a problem with any of your answers?"

"Now we're on the same page," Zane growled low as he devoured her mouth with deep, sweeping strokes of his tongue.

Callie responded ardently and eagerly, much to his delight. Her arms wrapped around his waist, pulling at his shirt until she made contact with bare skin. Her nails raked lightly over his back, and he groaned in pleasure. Zane held Callie tightly, and she molded her body against his. His cock throbbed almost painfully, and it was all he could do to stop from taking her right then and there on the floor.

Breaking the kiss and embrace, Zane fought to clear his head and cool off, a hard battle of its own.

"I'm sorry, I didn't mean to come on that strong. The last thing I want is to rush you." Zane ran shaky fingers through his short, cropped hair. He couldn't control himself around her. Callie was beautiful and tempting, more so than any female he'd ever met, and he'd never wanted a woman this much before.

Callie bit her lip as she searched his face. She reached for his hands, pulling him closer.

"I guess you weren't paying attention, but I'm reasonably sure I was right there with you." She caressed his cheek and Zane nuzzled her soft palm. "If I didn't want you to kiss me, you would know it. I have feelings for you, Zane, and I'm not scared to explore them."

His eyes shuttered closed for a moment as he took in her words.

"You mean it?"

"Every bit of it," Callie murmured.

Pulling her back into his arms, Zane reached up and undid the elastic from her hair. Waves of glossy chestnut hair tumbled around her shoulders and down her back. His hands dove into the silky tresses as his gaze drifted to her ripe lips, hovering for a moment before he claimed her mouth once again.

"Tell me you want me," he husked.

"Do I have to say the words?"

"Nah, I got this."

Scooping her into his arms, Zane headed for the large bedroom. He wasn't second-guessing himself anymore, and he sure as hell wasn't going to wait. His wolf would figure it out sooner or later. Zane wanted Callie like no other, and his feelings for her were growing stronger every day. They would explore those feelings together and see where they led.

Zane released Callie by the side of the bed, gracefully standing her in front of him.

"You're so beautiful," he choked.

Taking advantage of his hesitation, she gave a sultry smile.

"But I'm not fragile." Callie made short work of his shirt, dropping it to the floor. She kissed him hungrily while her hands were busy at his waistband, working the button and zipper.

Zane chuckled through the kiss.

"You may not be fragile, but you're precious to me, and I'll always treat you as such."

His words stopped her in her tracks.

"I've never known anyone like you. No one has ever told me that before." Callie's eyes widened in wonder.

"I would say they were all fools, but I'd like to think you had to wait for me to come into your life." Zane pushed his jeans down, kicking them out of the way. He faced Callie, who was still in shorts and a bikini top.

"I want to be the one you remember all your life, the one who imprints your heart."

His large hands cupped her ass and slid her shorts down, slow and sensually, skimming her silky-smooth legs. He breathed in her natural scent mixed with the remnants of sunshine and the outdoors. Wet heat flared between her legs, and Zane inhaled deeply, all his senses aroused to the highest of levels.

Zane explored her with his tongue, drowning in her taste. Callie arched against him, and Zane held her steady. She tasted like spiced honey and sin, and Zane was never going to get enough of her. In a smooth movement, he had them both in bed, turning Callie onto her stomach. His large, strong hands massaged her shoulders and back, then curved around her glorious, rounded cheeks. Spreading her legs, he eased inside her, a little at a time, slowly seating himself entirely. His movements were leisurely and teasing, drawing tortured moans from Callie's lips. Bucking beneath him, she begged for more, but Zane refused to hurry, though the strain was wearing on him. He fought his own release while he focused on covering every inch of her satin smooth skin with caresses and kisses.

Callie thrashed and moaned as Zane thrust harder and faster, the need to explode building like the force of a storm. She screamed her release, and Zane stiffened and convulsed, melting in her heat.

Zane rolled to his side, spooning against Callie. Their breathing eventually slowed, as did their erratic heartbeats. He idly massaged a rounded breast and lazily kissed her shoulder.

"Callie?"

"Hmm?"

"You okay?"

She gave a low, throaty laugh and rolled over to face him.

"You worry too much." Callie kissed him on the tip of his nose.

Zane pulled her on top of him and cradled her face with his hands.

"When it comes to you, I always will."

"I don't want you to worry about me. I don't want to be a burden of any kind to you. The last thing I want is to hurt you in any way, and I'm scared it's going to happen, no matter what."

The fear in her eyes was real, and it tore at Zane's heart.

He covered his eyes with an arm while Callie remained where she was, her head against his chest.

"I'm sorry if I get too intense. It's just how I am. What I feel for you is stronger than anything I've ever felt before. Part of it scares the hell out of me, the other part, I want to embrace. My wolf doesn't know what's going on, and that's another problem."

He gazed into her lovely brown eyes, so serious and full of concern.

"I'm half in love with you already, Callie. I'm not one to play games or dodge around emotions. I know in my heart, you're the one for me, and I'll do anything it takes to keep you safe. If I get hurt in the process, so be it."

"I want to believe we're mates, I truly do, but I'm broken, Zane. You deserve more… you need more."

His hands traced the contours of her body as he brushed his lips to hers.

"All I need is you."

Chapter 11

Callie couldn't remember the last time she'd been this happy, if ever, but she was scared, too. She'd meant what she'd told Zane—she was broken, and he deserved better than her or what she was capable of giving. She would never be able to thank Ridge for taking a chance on her, though she understood he was actually doing it for his brother.

Callie was worried about Zane's safety. Nephinae would make a move sooner or later, and she was cold-blooded enough to be capable of anything. Being honest with herself, she was more than a little surprised she hadn't heard from Rhistel yet. Her uncle had explained long ago that time worked differently in the fae realm, but she didn't know how to figure the difference or if it could even be done.

For now, she would do her best not to worry or fret about the future. If she couldn't change it, there was no sense in wasting time over it. Taking a deep breath, Callie tried to shake off the negativity and focus on the here and now... and that meant a new life with one very hot and desirable shifter.

"What are you doing, gorgeous?"

Zane's husky voice sent shivers up and down Callie's spine. Of course, those warm kisses on the back of her neck may have had something to do with it too.

"Working on our dinner. From the energy we've expended, we can't go to work on empty stomachs."

Zane turned her around, pulling her into his arms. Laughing, she managed to snag a dishtowel to wipe off her hands.

"Is that a complaint?"

Zane gave her a sly grin and Callie's heart fluttered.

"Not in the least." She nipped his bottom lip playfully. "Simply stating the facts."

Zane's growl was low and rumbled from deep down in his chest.

"Minx. Why do I get the feeling you're going to give me a run for my money?"

"Would you have it any other way?" Callie returned his growl with a sultry smile. Pushing him away before he could take their banter to the next level, she playfully slapped at his chest. "Don't you have something else to do? I have things to tend to before work this evening."

Zane pouted but was interrupted by a knock at the door before he could say anything else. Striding over to the door, he quietly conversed with the person a moment before opening the door and allowing several people into the house.

"Callie, I want you to meet these guys. This is Steve, Bixby, and Reg. They're Cole's team of enforcers and they'll be guarding the house... and you." Seeing Callie's arched brow, he hurried on before she could protest. "One of them will be inside with you if I'm not here, and the others will be patrolling the house and woods. This is non-negotiable." He draped an arm around her, pulling her close to soften his edict. "I need you safe, gorgeous."

Callie wasn't thrilled with the idea of guards or enforcers. Call it what you will, she would have someone watching over her every minute of the day. On the other hand, she knew Zane worried about her, so she would take that into consideration and do her best to deal with it.

After polite greetings and making sure she knew who was who, the team departed to make their rounds.

"I know you don't like the set-up, and we're going to try not to smother you, but I'm not taking any chances with your safety."

"I get that, Zane, and I appreciate it, I do..."

"There's a *but* coming," Zane joked.

"Yeah, I guess there is." Callie tried to smile, but it fell flat. "It seems the more we talk about it, the more of an imposition I am on you and your brothers." She made an exasperated sound. "On your whole pack, for that matter. It would be for the best if I left." Her voice dropped off to almost a whisper.

She flinched when she saw the flash of gold in Zane's eyes, but when she looked again, they were the deep blue she was used to.

"You can't run forever."

Callie lowered her head, torn between what her heart wanted and what she knew was the right thing to do. Zane was right—she couldn't keep running but staying would put Zane and the others in danger. Callie couldn't live with herself if anyone got hurt because of her.

Zane's finger gently lifted her face up to meet his gaze, and it was like looking in a mirror.

Everything she felt, she saw in his eyes. She was hurting him when she talked of leaving and, in turn, that hurt her even more.

"You said you'd give us a chance. Are you so quick to turn and run?"

Zane's soft-spoken words tore at Callie's heart, and tears streamed down her cheeks.

"I'm scared, Zane. I'm just so... scared."

Zane wrapped his arms around her, not saying a word, simply holding her while she cried. All her brave words, all her good intentions, washed away with her tears. Before meeting Zane, she'd followed her gut instincts without hesitation. Callie was lost now, and she didn't know what to do anymore.

"I know you're scared. I get that." Zane held her tight, speaking in a low, controlled voice. "I know you're worried about the danger you might bring to the pack. The part you don't know is Ridge has informed the pack of what's going on, so everyone knows what's on the line. We're all in this together, gorgeous. Every one of us will protect you. You're one of us now."

"But how can they do that? They don't know me..."

"They know enough, Callie. You've met most of them already. Everyone likes you, and believe me, they're all hoping you turn out to be my Fated

Mate. Nothing would make the pack happier, especially me."

"How are we supposed to know that?" Callie pulled back so she could look up at Zane's face. "With my wolf broken, there's no way of finding out."

"Ridge is setting up a meeting with Mancy. If anyone can fix your wolf, it will be her."

"Who's Mancy?"

"She's our pack healer," Zane explained. "She's also a medicine woman and traiteur.

"Traiteur?"

"It's French for faith-healer. There are still a few of them in the area, but Mancy is also a shifter, so her powers are much more forceful and effective."

"But, what about..."

"That's enough questions for now. You'll meet Mancy tomorrow and can ask her all the questions you want. She loves to talk and will gladly explain everything to you."

Callie stifled a groan. Zane was adamant about no more questions. They would have to wait. Apparently, Zane had other plans.

"How long before you finish what you're doing?" Zane asked, sniffing at the contents in the crockpot.

"Only a few more minutes. All I have left is to clean my mess. Why? What's up?"

"I need to go into town to pick up some packages for Dennis at the garage. I figured you could come with me, and we could have lunch."

"I'd like that." Callie was already mentally going through her closet and wondering if Zane would let her get in a bit of shopping while they were there.

"Good deal. I need to tend to the boat real quick, then I'll be ready. How about twenty minutes? That give you enough time?"

"I think I can manage it." Callie grinned as she cleared the counter and made sure the roast was on the right setting. "I'll meet you downstairs as soon as I'm done."

Callie could feel the tension ease as the Raptor sped down the highway. It probably had a lot to do with being on the move. Since she'd been on her own, Callie hadn't stayed in one spot for very long, always feeling safer on the road. As much as she liked living in Bayou Crescent, old habits were hard to break.

The bayou running alongside the highway was murky, but the activity surrounding the water was busy and charming. Fishermen worked on shrimp boats moored to small docks while life ran its course in the small communities. Smiling people waved at Zane as they passed, showing her he was well known in the area.

"Do these people know you're a shifter?"

"Not sure, to be honest. It's not discussed in the open, but there have always been rumors. We keep to ourselves but will help when it's needed. The pack has searched for lost kids and dragged more than one vehicle out of the bayou. People down here help each other, especially during storms and tragedies. It's how they are... humans and shifters alike."

"You don't see much of that anymore." Callie pried her gaze from the window, turning in her seat to face Zane.

"Not so much in the metropolitan areas, but the old ways still thrive in rural areas." Zane reached over and took her hand, squeezing it gently. "Feeling a little better?"

"Yeah," Callie admitted. "Guess I needed to get out for a little while."

"I figured it. Whenever you start to get antsy, talk to me. We can always take a drive or work out what's bothering you."

"Got me figured out already?"

"No," Zane replied. "But I want to get to know you better, and I can't do that if you're not here with me."

"I'm sorry."

"There's nothing to be sorry for, gorgeous. All I ever asked for was a chance."

"That's true, and I'm not holding up my end." Callie felt heat rise in her cheeks and nervously toyed with a lock of hair.

"You have a lot on your mind." Zane winked at her. "I need you to trust me."

"I do trust you, Zane... more than I've trusted anyone else. It's only my mind keeps playing an unending reel of worst-case scenarios. It's hard to believe in happy-ever-afters when you lead a life like mine."

"I get that." Zane linked their fingers together. "As long as you're here, I can deal with whatever life throws at me. I'm a man of simple needs."

"You make everything sound so easy." Callie sighed.

Her gaze drifted to the road ahead, and she gasped, her eyes widening in shock.

"Zane! Look out!"

The screeching of brakes filled the air as Zane fought to avoid hitting the wrecked vehicles blocking the road. Caught in the curve, the Raptor fishtailed, and Zane struggled not to hit the other vehicles or land in the bayou.

Punching buttons on the door panel, Zane lowered the windows, giving them an escape if they ended up in the water. The truck shook and wobbled as he attempted to regain control. Callie had a death grip on the grab handle when the truck turned completely around, sliding to a stop mere inches from the wreck.

Callie caught the dash with both hands and lowered her head against it. Breathing in hitches, she tried to get herself under control.

"Cal! Are you okay?"

Zane reached for her, running his hands over her arms and legs, looking for injuries.

"I'm all right. What about you?" Callie unsnapped her seatbelt and reached for Zane.

"I'm good, baby. Only worried about you."

"Are y'all okay in there?" A voice from the road called to them.

Callie looked up to see a worried-looking middle-aged man peering in at them through the open passenger window.

Zane opened his door and stepped out to speak to the man. Callie wasn't sure her legs were steady enough to hold her just yet.

"Callie? There's a young couple who were injured. I'm going to see if I can help, but they have a kid with them. Could you check on the little girl? She's screaming her head off."

Shaky or not, there was no way Callie could refuse. Together, they made their way to the wreckage. The screams of a child got louder as they neared the scene.

"Has 9-1-1 been called?" Callie looked around until she locked on a young woman on the side of the road cradling an injured arm and trying to hold a struggling child with the other.

"Yeah, but it's going to take a while. We need two ambulances, and the only available one is still in Bellerieve, so we're going to have to wait for a second one."

Glancing at the young couple, Callie could tell they were both in pain, but nothing seemed critical. The older man was bruised and shaken but sustained no other injuries that he could tell.

"Guess we better see what we can do to help." Callie smiled encouragingly at Zane.

Crouching before the mother and daughter, Callie introduced herself.

"Hi, there. I'm Callie, and I'm going to stay with you until help comes. Is that all right?"

"Thank you." The young woman grimaced as she tried to comfort the child. "I'm Chloe, and this is Miranda." Her smile was shaky, but her eyes showed relief and gratitude. "We call her Randi."

"Hey there, Randi. You've got beautiful blue eyes, and I love your curls. You're so pretty."

Randi sniffled but was paying attention to Callie. *Apparently, the little girl responded to compliments.*

"Would you let me hold you while Zane looks at your mama's arm?" Callie held out her arms, and Randi reached for her willingly.

Once the child was safely with Callie, Zane stepped in.

Kissing Callie on the cheek, he whispered, "Thanks, gorgeous."

Callie crooned to Randi as she watched Zane assess the parents' injuries. Sprinting to the truck, he returned with a large first aid kit. Setting a splint in place relieved some of Chloe's discomfort, going by the relief on her face.

"Callie, I need you to take the baby somewhere she can't see this. Brad's shoulder is dislocated, and I'm going to put it back in place."

Indicating she understood, Callie took Randi closer to their truck, chattering nonsense to the child the whole time. Her father would no doubt scream when the arm was set back in place, and she needed to muffle the sound from the child.

"Daddy!" Little Randi's eye's widened at the scream, and she immediately started crying and squirming, trying to get to her parents.

"Shh, it's okay. Zane had to fix your daddy's arm. Let's go see how he is." Callie held the child against her, running her fingers through the girl's silky curls.

"Daddy!"

"It's okay, brat. Daddy's okay." Brad gave his daughter a thumbs-up and Randi stopped crying. She struggled to be with her dad, so Callie released the child but showed her how to sit next to her dad without hurting his shoulder.

A few minutes later, sirens were heard in the distance.

"Thank goodness," Chloe murmured.

Two ambulances and a sheriff's deputy pulling up to the scene was a welcome sight for everyone. Zane filled the EMTs in on what he'd done as they secured their patients. It was a tight fit, but they managed to get the family in one ambulance, while the other driver was loaded into the remaining unit.

Zane and Callie gave their information to the deputy and were ultimately allowed to leave.

"I called a couple of wreckers to clear the vehicles, but you're not going to be able to get into town for a bit." The deputy explained with an apologetic shrug.

"Not a problem. We're headed back to Bayou Crescent." Zane draped an arm around Callie's shoulder and led her to the truck.

Zane started the truck and headed toward home, holding Callie's hand tightly.

"Dennis is going to have to wait another day for his parts. How about lunch at the diner instead?"

"Sounds wonderful," Callie said with a tired smile. "All of a sudden, I have no desire to go anywhere."

Chapter 12

Zane woke to find Callie propped up on an elbow, staring down at him, her soft hand running lightly over his chest.

"Morning, gorgeous. Something on your mind?"

"Yes and no." She leaned over and kissed his lips gently.

With a groan, Zane captured her in his arms, deepening the kiss. His cock throbbed against Callie's warm softness and all thoughts of conversation evaporated.

"Questions later. Right now, I need you," he whispered gruffly into her ear as he rolled them over.

Callie parted her legs, and Zane entered her heat with a single thrust. His strokes were slow, sure, and possessive, and every movement was a shared pleasure. Their bodies shuddered as they came as one, clinging to one another, not yet ready to come back to reality.

With a groan, Zane rolled to the side of Callie, her hand clasped in his.

"Now, what was on your mind?" Zane brought her hand to his lips, kissing and sucking each finger.

"Umm… I forgot?"

"*That's* what I'm talking about." Zane grinned devilishly.

Callie weakly slapped his chest.

"Don't get too cocky, mister."

"Ah, I see what you did there."

They collapsed in each other's arms, laughter filling the air.

"I can't have my lady lacking attention," Zane told her after they'd calmed down.

"I assure you, it's not ever a problem." Callie's smile was a satisfied one.

"I did want to ask you about your medical knowledge. I never got a chance yesterday with all the excitement."

"Yeah, it got a little crazy at the diner."

Ridge, Cole's team, and the garage had scanners set up, monitoring for auto wrecks along the bayou. They were always prepared to help, so when Zane and Callie showed up at the diner, everyone knew about the wreck and wanted details.

"I went to LSU and majored in medicine because of things like yesterday's wreck. The pack needed someone to help Mancy with emergencies and skilled in practical medicine, setting simple breaks, stuff like that. Shifters heal rapidly, humans not so much." Zane sat up in bed as he explained.

"So, you're a licensed doctor?" Callie's brows shot up in surprise.

"I don't make a big deal of it, but yeah." Zane narrowed his eyes at her. "Do you find it so hard to believe?"

Callie's laughter rang out as she sat cross-legged in front of Zane, reaching for his hands.

"Not hard to believe, simply unexpected. You're the most low-key physician I've ever met."

"Probably because I never intended it to be a profession, just a valuable tool."

"You're an amazing man, Zane Landry, and full of surprises."

He reached over and kissed the tip of her nose.

"Keeps you on your toes." Easing out of bed, he said over his shoulder. "How about some breakfast before we meet Mancy?"

"You get bacon duty. I'll get the rest," Callie called out as she dashed out the bedroom, stark naked.

Zane laughed softly.

Wolf, you better get on board fast, because I love that woman.

Zane pulled in front of an elevated cabin set farther back from the other homes and of equal distance to the woods and bayou. The healer liked her solitude. It was probably for different reasons, but Zane understood the sentiment. He and his brothers set up their homes the same way—close to the pack if needed but far enough away to give them privacy.

"Morning, you two! I've been expecting you." A tall, tanned woman laden with bundles of dried herbs smiled broadly at them. "Coffee should be done. Come on inside."

"Hey, Mancy, we appreciate you taking the time to see us."

As they approached the healer, Zane made the introductions.

"Callie, this is Mancy Pellegrin. Mancy, this is Callie Evans."

"I'd shake your hand, but..." She grinned as she gestured at her bundles. "Zane Landry, you know darn well I always make time for you boys."

"Can I help you carry some of that?" Callie asked.

"Thanks for offering but I've got it." Mancy's light blue eyes sparkled as she started up the stairs with Zane and Callie following.

Once on the deck, Mancy walked over to a table where a large wicker basket sat. She laughed lightly as she laid the herbs carefully into the basket.

"I'm always forgetting the basket up here, but in my defense, I didn't think so many would be dried already." Going inside, she gestured to her guests. "Callie, how do you take your coffee? I've got it all."

"Cream and sugar works." Callie looked around in awe as she answered.

Zane pulled out a chair for Callie, remembering the first time he'd seen Mancy's home. The kitchen counters were full of bottles of all sizes and colors, bundles of drying herbs hung from hooks in the ceiling all around the room, and there was always a big pot of something cooking on the stove. The living room proudly showed off her Native American heritage with paintings and finely crafted pieces.

"Anything you need for your coffee is on the tray on the table." Mancy set down three mugs of coffee with spoons. "If you don't see it, ask. I'll have it stashed somewhere."

Mancy took a sip and closed her eyes. "Good stuff."

She turned to Callie and Zane. "So, I know what Ridge has told me, but I want to hear it from the horse's mouth, so to speak. Callie, what happened to your wolf?"

Callie set her mug down, taking a deep breath.

"The short version is the queen of the fae bound my wolf."

"That's one hell of a version, short or not." Mancy snorted. "I know you can't shift, but can you feel your wolf at all?"

"Not at all. I haven't felt her presence since it happened. Nephinae... she's the queen, said she would unbind her if I entered her service at the Sidhe court, but I can't bring myself to do it. She was the one who was responsible for killing my mother."

Mancy's look of horror matched his own the first time he'd heard the story. This time around didn't go down any easier.

"I'm sorry for your loss. It couldn't have been an easy decision, regardless," Mancy offered.

"It wasn't, and my mind hasn't changed. Other than my uncle, I want nothing to do with the fae. But I want my wolf back if there's any way possible."

"Let me do a little research. I vaguely remember a story of a bound spirit animal. If I can find it, I may be able to fit it to our needs."

Zane's heart went out to Callie when he saw the light in her eyes and joy on her face. If only Mancy could make this happen, he'd owe the healer for the rest of his life.

"Don't get too excited yet, child. Even if I had everything I needed, we still have to wait for the next full moon, and that's not for another two more weeks."

"I can wait!" Callie beamed at them. "This is closer than I've ever been to being whole again. Thank you, Mancy."

"Is there anything I can do to help?" Zane offered.

"Not yet, but I'll let you know after I do a little homework." Mancy snapped her fingers. "Yes, there is something. Could you let Ridge know I'll need access to the last resort? I'll need to use the ceremonial burial ground on the full moon."

"It won't be a problem, but I'll let him know."

"That's the second time I've heard someone mention *the last resort*. Am I allowed to ask what it is?" Callie asked tentatively.

Mancy glanced at Zane, putting the ball in his court. The last resort was only known to the pack and wasn't spoken about freely.

"The last resort is a special place on our island. Only pack members know about it, and we keep it to ourselves. It's a small patch of land with a cabin and the ceremonial burial ground Mancy mentioned. The cabin is heavily warded from all forms of evil, physical and spiritual. Anyone who enters the cabin is fully protected from all entities... even their presence is undetected by anyone searching. As far as the burial ground is concerned, when our healer performs a ritual, like Mancy will do with you, she buries an artifact in the sacred earth."

"So, no bodies on the island?"

Mancy and Zane both laughed easily.

"None we've found yet."

Callie could hardly contain her excitement, and nothing could wipe the smile from her face. It had been so many years since she'd connected with her wolf. Being a hybrid, her wolf had been special. Not so much in looks, she blended in with the pack, but *her* wolf was stronger, had more stamina and speed than the others. Callie wondered what her wolf would be like now since her fae powers had grown and evolved.

"Feeling kind of good?" Zane asked as he opened the truck door for Callie.

"I am, and before you warn me about getting my hopes up, I understand the risks."

"I wasn't saying a word." Zane held his hands up in surrender. "You're a smart woman. You know what you're getting into. All I wanted to say was no matter what happens, I'm here for you. I know getting your wolf back is important. I can't imagine what you've gone through without her, but my feelings for you won't change because of it."

Callie blinked back tears. How had she gotten so lucky to find Zane?

"I love you, Callie. I want you to know now... before Mancy tries to unbind your wolf, before anything else happens. Even though my wolf hasn't said anything to me, he watches constantly, which tells me something... like he's waiting for his mate to appear."

"I don't know what I did to deserve you, but I'm grateful. I never dreamed I'd find a pack who would accept me, and the thought of finding a mate wasn't even on the table, but here you are. I love you, Zane. I love you more than you could ever realize."

Callie was sure they were entertaining Mancy with the kiss, but she didn't care. All she cared about was returning the kiss of the sexiest shifter she'd ever met— the shifter she loved above all.

Chapter 13

"Didn't expect to find you here this early," Ridge said as he carefully set down the case of alcohol. "Callie with you?"

"No, she's at home." Zane hurried on when he saw Ridge's brow raise at his response. "Bixby is with her in the house, the others are patrolling."

"Everything still quiet?"

"Yeah, almost too quiet, though Callie thinks the enforcers are overkill now." Zane opened one of the boxes, stocking the cooler for the night.

"It's up to you and Callie, but I've found when you let down your guard, that's when it all hits the fan."

"Right there with you, and Cole hasn't complained about the extra security detail, so I'm guessing he's on the same page."

"Life is good when y'all agree with me," Ridge said drily.

Zane snorted. His brother must be in high spirits. He didn't joke around much.

"Before I forget, Mancy wanted me to let you know she's going to need the last resort for the next full moon."

Ridge brought in three more cases before he replied. Zane was used to his brother's gaps of silence in their conversations. He'd get an answer, he simply had to wait for it.

"Mancy can help Callie with her wolf?"

"She's looking into it. Said something about hearing of a similar case. She's going to see if she can find more details."

"As it stands, the healer is our only hope." Ridge walked behind the bar and fixed a glass of iced water. "I spoke to Maddox yesterday about the fae. They don't play nice, and they're tricky. Going up against the queen is going to be rough."

"I figured as much. Add in the fact they live in another realm, and we have zero advantages," Zane pointed out.

"I'm curious as to what this uncle of Callie's is going to say when he decides to make an appearance. He could be our ace up the sleeve."

"Callie speaks highly of him, but she doesn't know how far he would go to help her," Zane offered. "We're talking evil fairy tale queen, only in 3D."

Ridge barked a laugh. "Sometimes you sound like Cole."

"Ah, hell, it's catching." Zane shared the laugh.

"Wash that off when you get home. I can't handle two of Cole. I need *some* common sense in the room besides me."

"Don't let Cole hear you say that." Zane glanced around to make sure their younger brother hadn't slipped in unnoticed.

"Yeah, we'd never hear the end of it." Ridge slapped the bar, stretched, then started gathering empty boxes. "That should hold us until the weekend. I'm going to check on the store and the diner, make sure their orders are up to date." Ridge started out the room, then stopped and turned. "Did Dennis get his parts from Bellerieve?"

Zane looked up from the ledger he was working on. "He did. Tansy and Destiny were going shopping, so they offered to pick the parts up while they were there."

"Good enough. I'm headed back to the house if you need me."

"Headed there myself..."

The door burst open, and Reg streaked toward Zane.

"Get to the house. Callie's in trouble."

Callie couldn't fault Bixby. He was trying to stay out of her way. Callie grinned as she plugged the vacuum cleaner into the hall outlet so she could reach the bedrooms. The burly shifter was trying to do his job, and to his way of thinking, that meant keeping Callie in his line of vision—all the time. He had no way of knowing Callie treated housekeeping as a workout. Earbuds in place, music cranked up, she danced her way through the house with poor Bixby tripping over cords as he followed her. At last, she decided to give the guy a break.

"Bixby, give it a rest. Sit down and read or something. I'm right here, and I'm not going anywhere."

"Sorry, but Cole was specific in his instructions. We're not to let you out of our sight."

Hands on her hips, Callie let out a huff of air in exasperation.

"What good are you in protecting me if you strangle yourself with a vacuum cleaner cord?

"I'm not going down that easy," Bixby smirked with a gleeful wink.

"It's your neck," Callie grumbled as she turned the vacuum back on.

Bixby was leaning against the door frame of the master bedroom when the portal appeared. Callie looked up in surprise to see Rhistel coming through with one arm raised. Before Bixby could take two steps, the fae had called up a sphere separating Callie and himself from the Enforcer.

Bixby punched, slapped, and threw himself at the translucent dome, but couldn't penetrate it. He could see them but couldn't get to Callie. She turned on her uncle in fury.

"What the hell, Rhistel? Was this necessary?"

As calm as always, the fae folded his arms across the chest as he watched the shifter futilely beat on the sphere.

"Apparently. The wolf appears quite violent."

"What do you expect? He sees you as a threat!"

Callie turned to Bixby, asking Rhistel over her shoulder, "Can he hear me?"

"If I allow it."

"Do you mind?"

Rhistel waved a hand, and Callie turned her attention back to the Enforcer.

"Bixby, I'm all right, I promise. He's not going to hurt me." She turned back to Rhistel. "You're not, right?"

"Of course not. I'm here to talk to you," Rhistel said archly.

She faced Bixby again. "He's here to talk, and that's it."

The shifter backed a few steps, his expression surly.

"I'm not leaving the fucking room." He reached for his phone. "And I'm letting Zane know what's going on."

Callie acknowledged the disgruntled shifter, then turned and faced Rhistel.

"Do you have to be so dramatic?" she fussed. "What's this about?"

"I said I would be back with the queen's reply. Have you forgotten?" Rhistel seemed amused, paying more attention to Bixby than to Callie.

"No, I hadn't forgotten, but that was a few weeks ago," Callie reminded him.

"Nephinae is determined to have you return to the Sidhe court." Rhistel apparently got bored with Bixby and faced Callie. "She refuses to return your wolf, however. It seems our queen doesn't trust you will keep your word."

"That's rich." Callie snorted derisively. "You did tell her I wasn't interested in her proposition?"

"I did, and we seem to be at an impasse." Rhistel looked at her in resignation. "You do realize this impasse won't last? If you continue to thwart her, she will force your hand. I don't wish you to come to any harm, niece. Your life in the court would be one of luxury and status." He glanced around the bedroom. "What do you have here... a temporary place with a pack who is not your own? How long do you think they will accept you with no wolf to call?"

That stung, and she knew Rhistel had done it intentionally. He wouldn't hurt her physically, but words were sharper than swords at times.

"Think, Calista! You're sharp, use that brain of yours. By defying the queen, you place your friends in danger. These shifters cannot hope to protect you from the fae. You must know that! Come with me and save us all trouble and bloodshed."

Rhistel's face was grave, etched in eons of battles and strife. He was being lenient with Callie, and she knew it. The fae would say he coddled her, and according to their ways, they would be right.

"Why do you ask this of me? You know how I feel." A single tear trickled down Callie's cheek.

"The queen is aware you have come into your full powers." Rhistel let out a long breath, as he stood with his feet apart and his arms behind his back.

Callie could see the general in him as he discussed plans in the war room with his counsel. Her uncle had a shrewd mind, which had kept him alive for more years than she could fathom.

"I don't even know what my full powers are," Callie confided.

"Which is the prime reason she wants you. You would have the best teachers to train you, marshalling your powers into a force never before seen."

"What specifically do you mean, 'never before seen'? What makes me so special?" The color drained from Callie's face as she began to fit the pieces together.

"Your hybrid blood, niece."

"Callie!" Zane's yell was almost a howl as he raced into the room.

"You don't have much time, Calista. Nephinae will not wait much longer."

In an instant, the sphere vanished, and Rhistel strode through the portal, leaving Callie with the weight of the world on her shoulders.

Chapter 14

Zane felt his world implode when he saw Callie and the fae together in the orb, or whatever it was. His shift was instantaneous as he leapt for the barrier separating him from the woman he loved, only to crash through nothingness as it, and the fae, disappeared in the blink of an eye. His wolf slammed against the bedroom wall, stunning him for only a second. Righting himself, he spun around searching for Callie. Standing in the middle of the room, she appeared devastated, and his heart broke for her.

Shifting, he grabbed a pair of jeans from the dresser and slipped them on before approaching Callie. He held his arms open for a moment before she fell in them, sobbing like she'd lost a cherished loved one.

Reg and Bixby gestured to Zane, leaving them in privacy. Zane knew they wouldn't go far, and they would tell Ridge and Cole what had happened. It was something he wanted to know himself, but he wasn't going to push Callie for details. She would tell him when she was ready. Right now, she needed comfort, and he was there for her.

Cradling her like a child, Zane lowered them to the floor. He held her against his chest, running his fingers through her silky-soft hair. Zane breathed in her scent, the exquisite fragrance that was only hers, the essence that linked him to her as no other could.

"She's not going to stop..." Callie hiccupped. "I have to go."

"Slow down, love." Fear clenched Zane's heart. He was afraid he already knew the answers, but he had to ask and hear her say them. "Who isn't going to stop and where do you have to go?"

Callie looked up at him, her long dark lashes clumped together by tears, big brown eyes glistening brightly.

"Nephinae," Callie whispered. "She means to have me in her service." She lowered her head. "I can't fight her, and neither can you. She'll send her guards, and they'll kill everyone. I can't let that happen." Callie choked back a sob. "I'm so sorry I got you involved in all this, Zane. Can you ever forgive me?"

"There's nothing to forgive, gorgeous. You're the best thing that's ever happened to me. I simply don't know if I can let you go... not without a fight."

"It's not worth it... *I'm* not worth it. Don't you see? She'll destroy everyone in this pack without blinking an eye. She's vicious."

His mind raced. There *had* to be a way. Zane knew Mancy could fix Callie's wolf, but she needed time. Unfortunately, Cal's broken wolf wasn't even a factor at this point. This fae queen wanted his female, and he couldn't let it happen, but he didn't know how to stop her either.

"The fae that was here... that was Rhistel?"

"Yes, he brought the queen's reply," Callie answered in a rush. "She refuses to return my wolf and insists I go to the Sidhe court and serve her." Callie trembled as she spoke, and Zane held her closer. "It seems my hybrid blood has enhanced my full powers, making me a very desirable weapon... one Nephinae covets."

"We could move you to the last resort. The fae wouldn't be able to touch you there." Zane hadn't realized he'd said the words out loud until Callie responded.

"And basically, make me a prisoner?" Callie exclaimed. "There's still nothing stopping her from wiping you all out. There's no way around it, Zane. I have to go."

"What else did Rhistel tell you?"

"Only that I was running out of time," Callie said sorrowfully.

"Let's find Ridge. We need a game plan."

Zane helped Callie up, and they made their way out of the room, coming to a fast stop in the great room. It seemed they didn't have far to go because Ridge, Cole, and the Enforcer team were making themselves at home in his living room.

"What's the score?" Cole asked as they approached.

"The fae queen wants Callie and will take us all out to get to her. Callie thinks she should go."

"Hmph!" Cole snorted. "Somehow, I don't see that happening."

"I know, right?" Zane bit out.

"All right, you two, simmer down," Ridge warned. "Maddox Ward wants us to meet him at his place. He thinks he has someone who can help Callie."

"Help in what way?" Zane asked. "Mancy's already working on a way to unbind her wolf."

"It's not about her wolf. Let's save the speculation until we get there," Ridge stated. "I've got The Den covered for the night, and the enforcers are going to patrol the pack." He pointed at Zane and Callie. "You two, Cole, and I are taking a ride to New Orleans." Ridge stood, facing Callie. "I know you think you don't have any options but don't underestimate us, Callie. We protect what's ours."

The ride was relatively fast and easy, taking a little over an hour to get to the NOLA Shifters headquarters. The ten-story brick structure had undergone a complete renovation when Maddox Ward bought it several years ago. Now, the building held eight floors dedicated to apartments, the top floor comprised offices of the NOLA Shifter headquarters, and the bottom floor held various restaurants and shops owned and run by the residents.

Zane had been here several times, and the whole infrastructure never ceased to amaze him. Being in charge of a pack of volatile wolf shifters was a challenge, even a small pack like theirs. He didn't know how Maddox handled not only a pack as large as he had but one of multiple kinds of shifters.

Bishop Callan met them at the door with a welcoming smile and a big hug for Callie. Zane tamped down his jealousy, reminding himself Callie and Bishop had been friends way longer than he'd known her.

When the white tiger shifter gripped Zane's hand in a firm handshake, he pulled him closer and whispered in his ear, "We've only ever been just friends, and I hear you two are hitting it off. She's special, wolf. See that you take care of her."

"You can count on it, and that's why we're here."

"Follow me, gentlemen"—Bishop winked at Callie—"and lady, I'll take you straight to Maddox."

The elevator swiftly took them to the tenth level, opening to a beautiful, tiled floor, walls painted a light gray contrasted by black molding, and lush green plants on either end of the wide hall. Bishop opened a door, ushering them in with a wave. The reception area followed the color scheme of the hall, giving a sleek and modern look to the offices. There was no waiting. The secretary gave them a friendly smile as Bishop walked past her to a hall of offices.

Maddox Ward sat behind a massive black L-shaped executive desk. Shelves and tables were all black against teal-colored walls. It wasn't precisely to Zane's taste, but it fit the NOLA Alpha perfectly—strong, modern, and elegant.

"Welcome! I trust the trip was uneventful?" Maddox stood, walking over to a sitting area with a sofa and leather chairs. "We may as well be comfortable while we talk. Can I get anyone something to drink? My bar is well-stocked."

Even though he owned a bar, it was a little early in the day for drinks to his liking, but Zane didn't turn down the whiskey when offered. He had a feeling they were all going to need one or two before this was all said and done.

A soft tap at the door, then it opened to the secretary and an older black man wearing a tailored black suit and top hat, carrying a large satchel, much like the old-time doctors used. Zane had no idea who he was but figured things would get interesting shortly.

"Come in," Maddox welcomed. "I'm grateful you could make it. Have a seat, please." Returning to the bar, the Alpha fixed another drink and handed it to the gentleman. "Now that we're all here, let me make the round of introductions. Everyone, this is Papa Moulin. He is a local voodoo priest and has offered to help us." Maddox hurriedly introduced the group to the priest, and everyone waited to hear what Papa Moulin had to say.

"Mr. Ward has explained the situation to me," the priest began, his voice soft and lilting. "If I understand correctly, Ms. Evans has a familial link to one of the fae, which is how she is located on this plane."

"Yes, that's correct," Callie acknowledged. "My uncle can locate me wherever I am at any time."

Papa Moulin pulled the satchel from between his feet and opened it. He withdrew several items, placing them on an end table next to him.

"I can sever the link—all I need from you, Ms. Evans, is a little of your blood. Are you willing?"

Zane tensed, but Callie seemed receptive to his request.

"Yes, of course."

Papa Moulin glanced up at Maddox. "If you would be so kind as to secure a chair for the lady next to me?" An armless chair was placed next to the priest, and Callie changed seats.

Zane noticed the roll of gauze and tape on the table and wondered exactly how much blood of Callie's would be required for this voodoo ritual. He wasn't comfortable with any of it, but it wasn't his call. If it protected Callie and she was amenable, so be it.

Papa Moulin gestured for Callie's hand, and he held it, palm up. Picking up a silver dagger, he sliced her palm, then turned it over, letting the blood drip into a small silver chalice. Callie winced when the blade cut through her flesh but otherwise didn't make a sound. When the priest was done, he efficiently wrapped Callie's hand with the gauze and tape, then went back to his preparations.

Several bottles and bags of ingredients were crushed and mixed with the blood as the old man chanted to whatever gods he believed in. When he finished the chanting, he reached once more into his bag and pulled out a silver pendant. With deft fingers, Moulin opened the pendant, releasing a tiny ampule. With an eyedropper, he filled the ampule with the blood mixture, resealing it tightly. Replacing the vial inside of the pendant, he closed it and handed it to Callie.

"Wear this at all times. It will sever the link, and your uncle will not be able to locate you so easily."

"I don't know what to say except thank you." Callie smiled gratefully.

"Your thanks are all that is needed, child. Don't forget, never take it off, even when bathing. If you do, the link is restored."

"I'll remember, I promise," Callie vowed.

Zane wasn't sure how to find out the priest's fee, but he knew the man expected payment. Out of the corner of his eye, he saw Ridge signal him.

Making his way to his brother, he arched a brow in question.

"Payment has been made," Ridge informed him.

"Consider it paying it forward," Maddox whispered, standing next to Ridge. "Papa Moulin owed me a favor. I simply passed it on."

Zane shook the Alpha's hand. "Thank you. Call me anytime and I'll make it good."

"I'm not worried, my friend. The Landrys always keep their word." Maddox chuckled lightly.

Chapter 15

Callie knew she wasn't out of danger and was well aware Nephinae wasn't going to stop until Callie was in the fae realm, but for now, she felt freer than she ever had. Zane and his brothers had come up with a plan on the drive home, and while Callie wasn't thrilled with part of it, she was smart enough to realize it was for the best.

Gathering what she would need for a few days, Callie threw them in the duffel bag, along with Zane's. He'd already packed and was outside, going over details with Cole and the enforcer team. Looking at the rumpled sheets on the king-sized bed reminded her of last night's lovemaking. A smile tugged at her lips as the memory played back in her mind. As always, Zane had been gentle and thorough, always making sure she'd been satisfied before he sought his own release.

Males like Zane were rare, and Callie counted herself as one of the lucky ones to find him. Her love for him was deep and strong, and she didn't want to imagine a life without him. She refused to think past today.

"About done, gorgeous?"

Callie was pulled from her musing by Zane's husky voice. Looking up, she hungered at the sight of him but knew this wasn't the time.

"I think I have everything. What about food? I don't imagine there's anything in the cabin."

"Everything's been taken care of." Zane wrapped her in his arms, kissing her tenderly on the forehead. "It's not going to be that bad... it's only for a few days, just enough to throw Rhistel off your trail."

"I hope this works." Callie forced a smile.

"We're going to give it our best." Zane gave her a lopsided grin as he reached for the duffel. "Let's head out. Our day is going to be full enough with getting settled in, and we both have to work tonight."

The sound of a truck horn propelled them into action.

"That's our cue." Zane captured Callie's hand in his. "Cole's taking us to the island, and one of the guys will pick us up this evening. It's best if the place looks like I'm still around."

"What about my car?"

"Taken care of... Dennis is going to lock her up in one of his bays," Zane explained patiently.

"Sounds like you have everything accounted for. I'm impressed."

"As you should be."

Zane winked at her in that cocky way she adored.

"You two coming, or you're gonna stand there and make googly eyes at each other all day?" Cole called out.

"Did he just say googly eyes?" Callie asked.

"Fairly sure that's what I heard." Zane flipped off his brother as they headed to his truck. "That's rich coming from the man-whore of Bayou Crescent."

"Don't knock my game. All the females make googly eyes at me, so I know what I'm talking about." Cole grinned and winked at Callie.

"Your ego is unbelievable, little brother."

Zane rolled his eyes, but the laughter assured Callie it was all done in fun.

"Get us to the island, bro. Far be it from us to get in the way of your game."

"Y'all are good. I don't have any plans until this evening. Tansy is meeting me at The Den."

"Tansy?" Zane arched a brow. "Didn't you already tag her?"

Cole snorted, and Callie covered her mouth to stifle the laughter. She'd learned quickly the brothers were a hot mess when they were together.

"What can I say?" Cole shrugged. "You treat them right, and they always welcome you back."

"I've got nothing." Zane conceded, lacing fingers with Callie. "I'll keep the one good one I've got. You can have all the others."

Callie smiled. She'd picked the right brother.

Callie entered the small cabin, dropped the duffel bag at her feet, and looked around in surprise. She wasn't sure what she'd been expecting, but it wasn't anything as nice as this. Exploring the room, her fingers trailed along the smooth wood of the hand-carved furniture. It was rustic, but a very well-taken-care-of rustic. Hardwood floors were bare of rugs, and windows were bare of covering, only the outside shutters giving them privacy. The running generator was the only sound on the quiet island, keeping the cabin air-conditioned with running lights and a fully equipped, functional kitchen. Running water was provided by the mainland's water system, pipework having been laid years ago.

"So, this is the last resort," Callie said softly, still walking around, taking it all in. Peeking into other rooms, she found two bedrooms and a bathroom between them. Efficient and functional in every way.

Looking closer, she found sigils over every window and door in the cabin. Those were probably the wards Zane had told her about, protecting those inside from all supernatural creatures. She hoped they were effective against the fae, or all this would be for nothing.

Zane walked up behind her, drawing her into his embrace and kissing the side of her neck. She melted at his touch, turned, and fell into his kiss. For a beautiful, magical moment, it was only the two of them, no worries, problems, or threats. How she wished she could make time stand still, right here, right now. He kissed her forehead and tucked a loose strand of hair behind her ear.

"Somehow, someway, I'll get this figured out, and when I do, it will be just us... forever," he growled low and urgently.

"I'm counting on it," she breathed against his chest.

All in all, it didn't take long to get settled in. The men had brought over food and provisions to last a week, and other than the one duffel bag, there was nothing else to unpack. The cabin had everything they would need. They spent the afternoon making love and napping, cherishing every minute spent together because who knew how long they had.

Callie woke to the smell of coffee and food. She looked up to find Zane setting a tray down on the dresser.

"Time to rouse yourself, gorgeous. One of the guys will be here in an hour to pick us up. Reality check... we have to work."

"You had to go and ruin it," Callie groaned.

"Come on, it's not that bad. We *do* work together." Zane's eyes twinkled with mischief.

"True, but it's not like we'll be alone." She pouted.

"Like that would stop me." Zane pounced on the bed and tickled Callie relentlessly. Shrieking with laughter, she begged him to stop.

"I can't breathe." She gasped.

"Sounds like I've got you where I want you." Zane husked in her ear.

"I thought we had to get ready for work?"

Zane groaned. "Now, who's the spoilsport?"

Laughing, they ate, showered, and dressed, with enough time to walk leisurely hand-in-hand to the dock. Callie felt good. She hoped tonight at The Den would be an easy one. Not that it was a bad place to work, but she didn't want anything to ruin her mood.

Glancing at the back parking lot, Callie saw Destiny and Kitty were already there. She liked the females and wished she had the opportunity to get to know them better away from work. Growing up on her own and on the move left little time for close friendships.

"You ready to rock and roll, gorgeous?"

Callie rolled her eyes but laughed heartily.

"You make it sound like The Den is a metropolitan club instead of a small shifter bar at the end of nowhere."

"You wound me." Zane clutched his chest, looking shocked. "I take pride in The Den. I started with only a simple country stop off..."

"Still there, my love." Callie was laughing so hard, she had to lean against the building to keep her balance.

"No respect," Zane closed his eyes and pinched the bridge of his nose. "Absolutely no respect around here."

"I'm sure you'll survive." Callie patted him on the shoulder, then kissed him on the cheek. "Let's see what we're in for tonight."

Going inside, the place was quiet except for low murmurings, clinking of bottles, and ice being poured into coolers. The Den wasn't open for business yet. Callie enjoyed these peaceful moments... the calm before the storm, Zane called them.

Going behind the bar, she acknowledged Ridge, waved to the females and Cole, then started at her station, making sure she had everything she needed for the evening. It was a weeknight, which usually meant just the regulars, the unmated males of the pack who were at loose ends and would rather hang out at the bar than go home to an empty house.

It hadn't taken her long to see that Ridge took care of his pack in many ways. It was because of the unmated males The Den offered a small menu, keeping them fed without having to cook for themselves or go to the diner. Large, mounted televisions played news and sports, while dart boards and pool tables gave them something to occupy their time until they were ready to go home.

This small shifter pack took care of each other and had accepted Callie readily, making her feel at home. They would never know how much it meant to her and how much she loved them all for that small act of kindness.

"It's quiet tonight. Doesn't look like we're going to have anyone else come in," Kitty said as she perched on a bar stool.

"Can't say I mind." Callie wiped the bar down more out of habit than need. "With everything else going on, I needed an easy night."

"How are you holding up? I heard y'all made a trip to New Orleans." Kitty balled up a napkin, then stretched it out again.

Callie had seen Kitty do that before. The female didn't like to keep still and was always moving. The napkin thing was a nervous habit.

"I got this." She held up the amulet. "A voodoo priest made it for me. It's supposed to sever the link between my uncle and me so he can't pinpoint my location."

Destiny and Tansy joined them at the bar, a beer in hand. Callie had a feeling they were going to close up early.

"Does it work?" Tansy asked.

"Don't know, to be honest." Callie shrugged. "I haven't seen him, but then again, his visits were never regular."

"Is it true you and Zane moved out to the last resort?" Destiny asked in a low voice.

Callie looked around to see if anyone was paying attention to their conversation, not that it mattered. They were all shifters with enhanced hearing, able to listen in at will. Still, there were customers in the bar, and Callie was cautious, so she nodded her answer.

As if sensing her discomfort, Kitty changed the subject.

"I think we need a shopping spree. You up for it, Callie?"

"A shopping spree?" She blinked, shifting gears in the conversation.

"Yeah," Tansy exclaimed. "We haven't done that in ages. Bellerieve or New Orleans?"

Callie glanced over at Zane, who was definitely listening to their conversation. Normally, she would never ask permission to go anywhere, but this was a different situation, and she needed his guidance. Zane walked over to their little group, draping an arm around Callie's shoulder.

"Don't mean to butt in, but can y'all make your trip local? We're not sure if the pendant works yet, and I'd rather Callie be closer to home, or... I can come with."

"Nope, no males." Tansy groaned. "Bellerieve it is."

"Not a problem, Zane." Kitty grinned. "We can make this work. How about we all meet here at nine tomorrow morning? It'll give us plenty of time to shop, and we can do lunch while we're there."

"Sounds like a plan." Destiny rubbed her hands together. "I could use a girl's outing."

"I'm looking forward to it," Callie added as she gave Zane a grateful smile.

They watched as the last of the customers left.

"How about we call it a night, ladies?" Zane asked. "Y'all can get in a couple of more hours sleep before your big excursion in the morning."

"Woot!" Destiny cried. "Let's lock this baby up!"

Chapter 16

Callie stretched and gradually opened her eyes. Her gaze fell on Zane, sleeping peacefully, all worries wiped from his face. She raised a hand to push back a stray lock of hair from his face and stopped herself. She didn't want to wake him yet, taking advantage of the moment to commit his face to memory. This was how she wanted to always remember him—the ruggedly handsome shifter who loved her.

In the short time since she'd met Zane, he'd given her more happy moments than she'd ever known. Callie didn't know if they were Fated Mates, but she couldn't imagine loving him any more than what she already did. He'd stolen her heart. For the first time, she'd allowed herself to think of a mate and the family they could raise together. They'd have beautiful pups—strong sons and maybe a daughter who would wrap her father's heart around her little finger. Callie realized how much she truly wanted a family with Zane.

Wiping away a tear, Callie was overcome with emotion. She needed Zane with an intensity that threatened to overwhelm her. Pushing the sheet aside, she smiled at the semi-hard erection. She was anxious to taste him, to take him into her mouth. She gripped the base of his cock and lowered her head. The bead of fluid at the tip was salty on her tongue, and she hummed in approval. She heard Zane groan at the same time he arched deeper into her mouth. Her tongue glided over his shaft in needy strokes, and his fingers knotted in her hair, working her head up and down his length.

Callie needed more, she needed him inside of her, needed him to fill her... to love her, as only he could. She straddled him, easing herself down, taking him in, her hips grinding against him. Callie was stretched, filled by his cock, and deep, steady strokes shook her. She rode him with a desperation, their merging bodies colliding with the wildest of passion. Zane rolled her over and slammed into her, rough and gasping. He was ruthless, driving deep and hard, and she met every thrust eagerly. She heard tortured moans, not totally realizing they came from her, as she cried out for Zane to come with her. Callie clawed his back and Zane made a low rumble of pleasure. They came together in shuddering waves, their bodies slick with sweat, chests heaving, clinging to each other, never wanting this moment to end.

"Caught up to you?" Zane asked in a hushed whisper.

That's when Callie realized how attuned she and Zane were to each other. He knew—he understood. She was so scared of losing him forever she was clinging to every moment they had together... and so was he.

"I didn't realize it until now," Callie confessed. "You're my world, Zane."

"You're my world too, gorgeous." Zane held her tight, fingers spiking through her long hair. "I love you more than I thought I could love anyone. Losing you would kill me." He kissed her like he'd made love to her, rough and full of passion.

"Promise me you'll be careful today." He fingered the pendant around her neck. "Make damn sure this stays in place."

"I will, I promise."

"Guess we better run through the shower." He picked at a damp, limp lock of her hair, letting it drop. "You're a hot mess right now."

Callie arched a brow at him.

"Is that a complaint?"

"No, ma'am. I'll take one of those every morning." Zane snickered. Sliding out of bed, he told her, "I'll get the water running and put the coffee on."

"You're forgiven." Callie smirked as she threw a balled-up t-shirt at him.

Zane insisted on staying with Callie until the others showed up, and she couldn't hold it against him. He was worried but doing his best to give her the freedom she needed. When Destiny pulled into the parking lot, Zane bent her over in a long, passionate kiss, much to the delight of the females who filled the air with whistles and cat calls.

"They're as bad as horny males," Zane muttered in the middle of the kiss, which of course, made Callie giggle, ending the kiss.

"Take care of my female, Destiny. I want her back in one piece," Zane growled as he opened the back door for Callie.

"Yes, Beta! We'll take good care of her." Destiny saluted with a saucy smile.

Callie knew Zane would watch them until he couldn't see the SUV anymore. He was territorial and possessive, but he was hers, and she wouldn't change a thing about him.

"All right, ladies," Kitty clapped her hands to get their attention. "What are we shopping for? That way we can form a plan and not waste a minute wandering around."

"Ordinarily, I'd gripe about Kitty and her plans, but today it makes sense," Tansy said agreeably. "Have to make the most of the time we have."

"I knew you'd see it my way sooner or later."

The laughter was infectious, and it stayed with them all the way to Bellerieve.

"Callie, are you giving any thought as to what you're getting Zane for his birthday?" Kitty asked.

"Crap, when is his birthday?" Callie's eyes widened in horror. "We never told each other our birthdays. Do I have time to get him something?"

"Calm down, girlfriend," Tansy patted her on the leg. "You're good. His birthday is June twenty-first." Tansy glanced toward the front seat. "That's right, isn't it?" Bobbing heads assured her she had the date right.

Callie sat back and tried to stop worrying. She *did* have time. She'd need it to figure out what to get him. It had to be special.

"I have *no* idea what to get Zane," Callie moaned. "I think I know him, but this gets thrown at me and I realize I don't know him at all."

"Girl, don't work yourself up." Destiny soothed. "It's always hard buying a gift for a new partner. You'll know it when you see it, and we'll help you."

"Thanks. With everything else going on, a birthday gift was the last thing on my mind." Then it hit her. Would she even be around for Zane's birthday? By then, she'd probably be in the fae realm. Determined not to get bogged down by Nephinae and her demands, she vowed she would buy Zane a gift regardless and give it to one of the girls to deliver it to him on his birthday.

"I think we should start with the mall," Kitty suggested. "I want a couple of outfits, and the mall has a few new boutiques. There's also two or three jewelry stores Callie can check out for Zane's gift."

"Don't forget that huge outdoor sports store," Tansy offered. "Every guy in the pack drools over the place."

"Sounds like a plan," Callie said, satisfied she'd have a good start. "Do they have a lingerie store like Victoria's Secret?"

Laughter rang out. "Hell, yeah!" All three women cried out at the same time.

"This is going to be a blast," Kitty announced.

Callie was surprised to see such a huge mall in an otherwise mid-sized town. The girls informed her at one time the mall's business had died off to almost nothing, then some big business took over, revamped the whole place, and brought in big-name stores, bringing life not only to the mall, but to Bellerieve, as well.

"Wow!" Callie exclaimed. "This place is huge. Where do we start?"

Tansy pointed straight ahead. "Through those doors and whatever catches our eye first."

"Works for me." Destiny hooked her arm through Callie's. "Come on, ladies. Shopping awaits us."

Laden with shopping bags, Callie was ready for lunch. Her stomach grumbled, acting like she hadn't eaten only a few hours ago. Making the corner, she saw a jewelry store.

"I'm going in there. I have a feeling," Callie called out to the others.

"You go ahead," Destiny told her. "We're going to sit on this bench right outside the store and wait for you. Take your time."

"Not too long, though," Tansy added. "Lunch is next."

Callie gave her a thumbs-up and wandered into the jewelry store. Halfway down the counter, she saw it.

"May I help you, Miss?" an eager young man asked.

Callie smiled as she pointed at the piece on display.

"Is the cross silver or white gold?"

"The cross is platinum. Would you like to see it?"

"Yes, please." Callie mentally did a fist pump. Silver would burn like hell. Platinum was ideal.

The cross was perfect, masculine with an attractive trim around the edges. Turning the cross over, Callie ran a finger over the smooth surface.

"We can engrave anything you'd like on the back... your name, a symbol. Our engraver is quite creative."

"A symbol? Like a crescent moon?" Callie felt her excitement rise. She had a feeling she'd found what she was looking for.

"I don't see where it would be a problem. One moment and I'll get Andre, our engraver."

"Thank you." Callie didn't wait long before the young man returned with another gentleman appearing to be in his mid-forties.

"Hello, I'm Andre, and I understand you'd like special engraving done?"

161

"Yes. This young man told me you could engrave a symbol, and I was wondering about a crescent moon."

Andre studied the back of the cross, pulled out a pen, and bent over the counter where Callie could see.

"I could put the crescent here in the middle. Would you like your name or initials?"

"You could fit it on there?" Callie didn't see how he could engrave on something so tiny, but he assured her it was possible.

"Will you be in the mall for another hour?" Andre asked.

"Yes, my friends and I are going for lunch."

"I don't have any other engraving jobs today. If you come back in an hour, it will be ready, and you can take it home with you."

Elated, she explained what she wanted, paid for it, leaving her cell phone number with him in case he needed to call. Callie rushed out of the store to tell the girls her good news.

Laughing and chattering, Callie and her new friends weaved through the throng of shoppers to a small Italian restaurant they'd seen earlier. A lively discussion ensued around the menu, but there was no debate on the wine. Callie felt like she'd earned it.

After a delicious and leisurely meal, Callie eagerly headed back to the jewelry store. Once she'd picked up the cross, her shopping spree would be complete. She'd found a couple of outfits and a handful of sexy lingerie sure to get Zane's attention. Callie was debating on which one she would wear later tonight when she arrived at the jewelers. Andre was waiting for her, a smile on his face and a small bag on the counter in front of him.

Hurrying over, she was practically breathless with excitement. Andre laughed lightly and opened a small box, presenting it to her.

The cross was beautiful, but it was the engraving she wanted to see. Turning it over, her breath caught. Not only had he engraved the moon but had antiqued it as well, so it stood out prominently. The left cross bar read *Yours Always,* and the other side read simply *Callie.*

"It's exquisite," she exclaimed. "Do I owe you extra for the antiquing?"

"No, ma'am," Andre assured her. "I thought it was a nice touch and took it upon myself."

"Thank you, Andre. It's perfect."

"It was a pleasure doing business with you. Please come again."

"You can count on it." Callie's smile was brilliant as she left the shop. Zane would love the piece; she was sure of it.

After showing it to the girls, it was unanimous. The cross was a win, and they were all shopped out. Callie couldn't wait to get back to Bayou

Crescent. She needed to stash her lingerie so Zane wouldn't see them until she wore them. The cross was another obstacle.

"Kitty, could you hold on to Zane's cross for me? I don't have a place to hide it while we're at the cabin."

"Not a problem." She slipped the box into her purse. "It will be nice and safe until you need it."

"Thanks, that's a big help." Callie gave a thumbs-up. "It's going to be hard enough hiding the lingerie from him. I want to surprise him... one outfit at a time."

"Girl, it's a good thing he's a shifter. A human would have a stroke."

The women got jostled more than once as they worked their way through the crowd, trying to get to their exit. Laughing and talking, they never noticed the trio of men closing in on them. Rushing them, Destiny, Tansy, and Kitty were knocked to the floor, packages scattering in all directions. Hurrying to their feet, they gathered their belongings and looked around.

"What in the hell was that all about?" Kitty swore.

"Did any of you see exactly what happened?" Destiny dusted off her jeans and juggled her bags.

"Where's Callie?" Tansy asked.

Kitty blanched, not wanting to let her mind go there.

"We have a problem," Destiny said in a shaky voice. Tansy and Kitty turned to see what she meant. Dangling from her outstretched fingers was Callie's pendant. "I found it in one of Callie's bags."

"Callie?" Tansy cried out.

Callie was nowhere to be seen.

Chapter 17

Zane pulled out his phone and checked the time again. Only five minutes had passed since the last time he'd checked. They should've been back by now. Every one of those females was responsible and always early for work. If they'd been in an accident, they would've called. So, where were they?

The SUV pulled into The Den's lot and Zane exhaled a long whoosh of air. He usually wasn't the worrying kind, but this was Callie, and these weren't normal times. The vehicle pulled up to where he was standing and stopped. Destiny, Kitty, and Tansy exited, fear etched on each face. Zane's heart tightened.

"Where's Callie?" His voice was raspy, and he tried again, this time louder.

"Where's Callie? Someone better start talking, and fast!"

Kitty stepped up, her eyes red and swollen from crying.

"She's gone, Zane. They took her."

"Gone. What do you mean, gone?" Zane stabbed at his hair and stared at the sky for a moment. "How in the fuck did that even happen?" he roared.

Kitty trembled but stood her ground while Destiny and Tansy quaked behind her, both females openly crying.

"We were leaving the mall when we were rushed by some guys. They knocked us down, scattering our bags everywhere. By the time we'd picked everything up and looked around, Callie was gone." Kitty took a step forward, then apparently thought better of it, remaining where she was. "We looked everywhere for her. We couldn't pick up her scent, Zane. I'm so sorry." Kitty fell to her knees, sobbing. "I'm so sorry, Beta."

"What about the pendant?" Zane had a death grip on his control, fighting the urge to tear out their throats on the spot.

"I found it in one of her shopping bags, Beta," Destiny said in a soft voice. "She was wearing it, I swear! I don't know what happened or how it got there."

Zane glared at the three females, daring them to move. Pulling out his phone, he speed-dialed Ridge.

"We've got a situation. I need you and Cole at The Den... ASAP."

"We're on our way."

Zane ended the call, turned, and unlocked the front door to the bar.

"Let's go inside, ladies. We need to go over this." Not looking to see if they followed, Zane went inside... straight for the whiskey.

He knocked back two fingers of whiskey and decided the bottle was faster and easier. He was taking a long pull when Ridge and Cole stormed in.

Ridge side-eyed Zane, then looked over at the females before he said anything.

"What happened to Callie?"

Using the whiskey bottle, Zane pointed at Destiny, Kitty, and Tansy, huddled together at a table.

Ridge walked over to the women, straddled a chair, and stared at each one of them. The fear on their faces was stark, so the Alpha knew this was dire. These women were strong and fearless. Whatever had happened was not going to be good.

"I'm going to assume a search party isn't going to help," Ridge said softly.

"No, Alpha." Kitty dabbed at her red-rimmed, swollen eyes with a napkin. "She... they... Callie vanished into thin air. She was there one minute, then she was gone."

"We were careful, Alpha," Destiny cried. "She was wearing her pendant, we all made sure of it, but then we found it in one of her bags. I swear we don't know what happened."

Ridge rubbed his chin as he processed what he'd been told. He turned to Tansy, who was dry-eyed but obviously in a state of shock.

"Tansy, can you tell me what happened? Tansy?"

The woman slowly turned to face her alpha, her eyes wide and unblinking. She nodded once.

"We... we went to the mall. We shopped, then had lunch. Everything was fine... we were getting along great, laughing and joking." Tansy took a deep breath. "After lunch, Callie had to pick up one last thing, then we headed to the car. The mall was really crowded, all the stores were having sales, and we had to weave through the people to get to our exit. Then these men rushed us, knocking us all down. Our bags flew out of our hands... it took us a few minutes to gather them and make sure everything was still there. That's when we realized Callie was gone... and Destiny had found Callie's pendant."

"Did any of you get a look at these men?" Ridge asked.

All three shook their heads.

"They came at us from behind, Alpha," Kitty said. "We never saw more than a glimpse."

"How in the fuck are we supposed to handle this," Cole bit out.

"I'm not sure yet." Ridge turned to the women. "Why don't y'all go home and get some rest? I'll get someone else to work the bar tonight."

"If you don't mind, Alpha, we'd rather work," Kitty offered.

Destiny agreed without hesitation.

"I can work the bar in Callie's place," Tansy offered.

"I appreciate it, but only if y'all are sure."

"We'll be back as soon as we unpack and change."

"Want me to get the team to man the bar tonight?" Cole asked.

"Yeah, the three of us need to work this out."

The women filed out, but not before approaching Zane and once again offering their apologies. Zane couldn't blame the women, they hadn't done anything wrong, and there was nothing they could have done—he knew it deep down.

His eyes burned like fire, and it took him a minute to realize it was because of the tears. He dashed at his eyes. He couldn't even remember the last time he'd cried, if ever.

"It wasn't your fault, any of you. I'm sorry I jumped down your throats."

The women stepped closer, and Zane held all three of them. No one could tell whose tears belonged to who, they all flowed the same.

Callie squinted through the darkness. She could hear the rustle of movement but couldn't make out anything.

"Who's there?" Her voice was scratchy and raspy, she almost didn't recognize it as her own.

"Believe me, you're better off not knowing." The weakened voice came from her right, a small distance away. The sound of chains clinking sent a shiver through her.

"Tell me," Callie demanded. "Is this the fae realm?"

"Where else wou—Merciful Lady... Calista, is that you?"

"Rhistel?" Callie swallowed hard. The worst had happened—Nephinae had made good on her threat. "It's me. Where are we?"

"The queen's dungeon."

"Dungeon? Why? Why are *you* here?" Callie tried to move closer to Rhistel's voice but found herself shackled to the wall by an ankle. Metal cuffs had been placed on each wrist, but Callie had no idea what their purpose was.

"Nephinae ordered me to open a portal to you. She didn't believe me when I told her I was unable, so she had me placed here."

"I had an amulet made, it severed our link," Callie confessed.

"Mystery explained."

"Is this the queen's idea of a life of luxury and status?" Callie bit out.

"She took her anger at me out on you, I'm afraid."

"This is hardly endearing her to my heart." Callie pulled as hard as she could on the chain, but it was strong, not giving an inch. She felt around the wall, finding the plate firmly bolted in. She wasn't getting out of this without a key. "Does she actually think I'll be a willing subject after this?"

"Do either of us have a choice, child?"

A door creaked open, and the stomping of feet approached. A flare of light blinded Callie temporarily and she shaded her eyes with a hand.

"Girl! The queen wants to see you. Get up!"

Callie listlessly got to her feet, then fell back against the wall when a bout of lightheadedness hit. The guard grabbed her arm and shook her, which didn't help her stand any better. Another guard unlocked the manacle around her ankle, and they dragged her from the room.

By the time they reached the throne room, Callie was weak and exhausted. The guards let go of her and she fell to her knees.

"Leave her, it's where she needs to be when the queen arrives," one of the guards muttered.

Callie couldn't understand why she was so weak and listless, not that she could remember much since being knocked down at the mall. She wondered about the girls and how they had broken the news to Zane. He would be furious, especially because he had no way to come after her.

A rustle of movement pulled Callie from her thoughts. Looking up, she saw a slender, woman wearing a flowing black gown and a cloak of iridescent black feathers approach the throne. A crown of black spikes sat atop long spirals of blonde hair. Nephinae, Queen of the Sidhe court.

"So, this is the hybrid." The queen's voice was cold and haughty, much like her appearance. "Rise, girl, so I may see you."

Callie tried to rise but fell back weakly. When she tried again, a guard grabbed her arm and pulled her up.

"I must say I don't know what all the fuss is about." Nephinae canted her head to one side, then the other, studying Callie. "I think I wasted a lot of precautions on you."

Deciding to be safe rather than sorry, Callie remained silent. This was one of the times she regretted Rhistel not telling her more of this realm, especially about Queen Nephinae.

"You will be put through a battery of tests to judge your skills and powers. When the Masters discover your strongest strengths, you will be trained and honed to become my weapon."

"And if I refuse?"

Icy blue eyes stared down at her, a slash of red lipstick smirked.

"Refuse?" Nephinae laughed harshly. "Did you not see Rhistel? That was simply for lying to me."

"He didn't lie to you," Callie screamed.

The queen froze in place.

"He told you the truth. He couldn't locate me. I had a magical amulet that severed our link."

"Well, well... perhaps those precautions were needed after all." The queen studied her nails for a moment. "Guards! See that Rhistel is released!" She turned her attention back to Callie.

"See? I can be fair, but you will have to earn your place at my side. Those braces you wear nullify any magic you possess. With your wolf bound and no powers, you are defenseless. Oh, and the iron you are chained to keeps you weakened... not as much as if you were full fae, but enough." She clapped her hands. "Take her back, I'm done with her for now."

Callie was dragged back to the dungeon, but this time, she was locked in a cell. She took advantage of the light the guard's torch provided, scanning the small area. A thin blanket, loaf of bread, pitcher of water, and a bucket had been left for her. It didn't take rocket science to figure out what the bucket was for.

The guard pushed Callie, and she stumbled, catching herself against the wall. Darkness prevailed when the guards left. Feeling around for the blanket, Callie wrapped it around her the best she could as she leaned against the wall. Tears trickled down her cheeks, and she did nothing to stop them.

She missed Zane with all her heart and soul, and it was a hard realization that she would never see him again.

Chapter 18

Zane sat at the bar, staring at the empty bottle of whiskey. Damn shame shifters couldn't get drunk... freakin' metabolism. It was probably just as well, Zane didn't think there was enough whiskey in the place to get him where he wanted to be—numb and oblivious.

"Go to the island, brother. Run 'til you can't go anymore. Cole and I will be right behind you."

Zane closed his eyes. He'd heard Ridge speak like that hundreds of times to pack members. The Alpha's soft Cajun cadence was calming, but it also brooked no disobedience, and right now, Zane was a member of the pack.

He slid off the barstool and gave a terse nod to his brothers, not looking their way. He didn't know if he could, without losing the last vestige of control he was clinging to.

Zane didn't think and did what he was told— drove to the landing, parked his truck, and jumped in the boat moored at the pier. Zane wasted no time getting to the island. He secured the aluminum hull, stripped, threw his clothing in the boat, shifted, and ran as if the hounds of Hell were after him.

With Callie's disappearance weighing on Zane's soul, he was especially grateful for his wolf counterpart. The beast didn't need to think things through or analyze. He operated on instinct alone—he either fought or ran.

Zane shut down, letting his wolf have complete control. Ordinarily, he would have never done it. In his current state of mind, it would be too easy for his wolf to go feral, and there would be no coming back. His wolf had never acknowledged Callie was their mate, so, while he understood Zane was in pain, it wasn't *his* pain.

The sound of paws running hard reached Zane, ears perked forward to pick up any other activity, and while he recognized Cole's yip, and the low snarl of Ridge, he didn't feel like socializing, instead bounding off to the center of the island, where it was more heavily wooded.

Sometime later, chest heaving from running long and hard, Zane's black wolf came to a stop by a small running creek. The cool, crisp water slaked his thirst, refreshing one need while his senses tuned in to another need—hunger.

The predator was uncannily fast, lunging at him seconds after he registered the sound of something crashing through the brush. A yelp of distress was all the black wolf managed as he was sent tumbling across the hard ground. Scrambling to his paws, he immediately recognized the chestnut-colored wolf, whose normal green eyes now blazed a fiery gold. To his right, another wolf stood and watched. Snarling a warning, he squared off, ready to take on both wolves if pressed, even though he knew them as brothers.

"Zane, shift!"

The black wolf's lip curled back, fangs exposed. He recognized the name, but it wasn't his, it belonged to his human... and he wasn't here. The red wolf was circling him, looking for an opening, but he was smarter than that. They'd caught him off-guard once, it wouldn't happen again.

He growled, warning them to keep their distance. His human wanted solitude, needed time to heal, and he was here to protect him. The wolf knew it had something to do with the female, but he didn't understand everything yet. His human was attached to her and mourned her loss, but nothing called to him.

"How do we handle this, Ridge?" The red wolf had shifted. Cole. "I don't want to fight him, but he's practically feral. I don't get it. Callie isn't his mate."

"We don't know that, but Zane feels it." Ridge stared at him but didn't threaten. "Let's go home."

"You want to leave him here? No disrespect, but is that wise?"

"He'll be fine. Zane needs time. We can give him a little. The only way he can leave the island is if he shifts. I need you to get Mancy. I'm going to call Maddox. With enough of us working together, we'll figure this out."

Rhistel cautiously walked around the home where Calista had last been staying. It appeared to be empty, which left him in a bit of a quandary—remain here and wait for the one called Zane or search for the brother and alpha of the wolfpack.

Once Nephinae had released him, there had been only one opportunity to speak to Calista, and he'd garnered all the information he could from her. The Sidhe court was no place for one such as his niece. A hybrid, with both sides equally lethal, didn't change the fact she was a gentle creature. Calista didn't know the ways of the Sidhe, and they would take advantage of her sweet nature, destroying all the good in her. He couldn't let that happen. Rhistel had been unable to help Calista's mother—his own sister—but vowed he would not fail the only blood kin he had left.

Leaving the house and sifting through the woods, Rhistel watched the home of the alpha from a stand of trees. Even though he was not in the open, he felt vulnerable. A fae with eons of military training, he was astute enough to know a pack of wolf shifters were formidable opponents. He needed to be stealthy and smart about how he approached the alpha. He needed help to free Calista. It wouldn't serve her if he was incapacitated from the start.

"You better have a good reason for being here or this iron poker I've got pointing at your heart will pierce it before you can pull up that portal of yours."

Rhistel silently cursed. He'd seriously underestimated the shifter... a fledgling's mistake. To make matters worse, the alpha was aware iron was lethal to the fae. This one was formidable indeed.

"My name is Rhistel. I'm here on behalf of Calista. I am searching for the ones known as Zane and Ridge."

The shifter stepped around Rhistel and faced him.

"I'm Ridge, Alpha of this pack."

Another male stepped out from the woods to stand next to Ridge, while three wolves closed in around him. Rhistel shook his head in disgust. Five shifters had outsmarted him in an instant.

"Calista has been imprisoned by the fae queen. I need help to free her."

"Why should we trust you?" Ridge's question was more of a growl. "How do we know Callie is even alive?"

"You will have to trust me on the latter. Calista is my deceased sister's daughter, and she's the one who sent me here. She told me your name and where I could find you." Rhistel searched the group surrounding him. "Which one of you is Zane? I have a personal message from Calista."

The male standing next to Ridge growled, tensing as if ready for battle, and the alpha calmed him with a hand on the man's arm.

"Zane isn't available. Your message will have to wait."

Rhistel narrowed his eyes at the alpha, trying to decipher the terse response.

"What do you mean… not available? Did something happen to him?"

Ridge didn't answer right away, obviously deciding on how much or what to tell him. Rhistel could respect that. As leader, his duty would be to protect his pack, more so when it was one of his brothers.

"Come with me. We'll discuss this further in my home."

Ridge turned and walked away, surprising Rhistel that he was being trusted enough to do as the alpha wished. The fae side-eyed the trio of wolves—or perhaps trust had nothing to do with it. Rhistel followed the shifter.

Once inside the home, Rhistel saw yet another side to the alpha shifter. Ridge treated him as a guest in his home, the pack members showing him respect, even though he was surely seen in a suspicious light. The fae would have never been so lenient if the situation had been reversed.

Rhistel's gaze settled on a woman, sitting quietly in a corner of the room. She was thumbing through a thick book with more books stacked next to her. The woman spoke to no one and was left alone to her reading. She was attractive for a shifter, then he noticed the unusual tattoo on the side of her face. A detailed leaf extended halfway up her forehead and ended on her high cheekbone. He wondered who she was and what her part in all this was.

"Tell me your plan and how we're supposed to help Callie."

Once again, the alpha had eased up to him without him noticing. Either he was losing his touch, or this shifter was a phenomenal hunter.

"Shouldn't we include your brother, Zane, in this conversation? My niece is very much in love with him. I would think he should be a part of this."

"Do you know the way of shifters, Rhistel?" Ridge pulled up a chair to sit beside the fae.

"I'm afraid I don't know much about your people. I've kept to my realm, only venturing out to visit my sister, then to check on Calista now and then."

"I'll try to break this down for you. Wolves mate for life. As wolf shifters, we're a lot like them. If we're lucky, we'll meet our Fated Mate. There is only one for us, and that love will last our lifetime, but it's our wolf counterparts who recognize our mate first."

"But Calista's wolf is bound..." Rhistel connected the dots swiftly.

"That's where the problem lies," Ridge finished for the fae. "Zane's wolf can't sense Callie's wolf, so they don't know if they're Fated

Mates, yet they've fallen in love. When Callie was taken, Zane was unable to go after her, virtually helpless, and that's not something a strong shifter like Zane is used to feeling. He's in mourning, Rhistel... almost the same as if his mate had died. He let his wolf take over because he can't handle the pain, which is fine for now, but we don't have much time."

Rhistel looked at the alpha sharply.

"What do you mean?"

"If Zane doesn't shift soon, his wolf will go feral, and Zane won't be able to shift back. Cole and I will lose our brother."

"Is there a way for me to speak to him? If I could give him Calista's message, it would get through to him."

Something deep inside Rhistel told him he needed to have Zane with him when they attempted to rescue Calista. He hadn't told Ridge yet how weak Calista was from being chained in silver and iron. The combination of metals was killing his niece. He *needed* Zane, for Calista's sake.

"It might work," Ridge said approvingly. "Cole, get a couple of boats ready. We're going to the island to get Zane." He gestured to Rhistel. "We'll talk about rescue details on the way."

Rhistel relaxed a little. At last, they were getting somewhere.

Chapter 19

Rhistel gave the two small boats dubious looks. He was familiar with the concept—there were literally easier ways to travel.

"What's your problem, fae?" Cole smirked. "Can't swim?"

"Your question doesn't instill any confidence in your choice of transportation."

Ridge looked up from the engine he was checking over.

"You have a better suggestion?"

"As a matter of fact, I do. I can pull up a portal to accommodate all of us."

Two of the wolves, now shifted to human and introduced as Steve and Reg, growled low.

"Let's hear the man out," Ridge cautioned, as he jumped lightly to the pier.

Rhistel observed approvingly as the pack members settled down, acceding to their alpha.

"It's how I travel to this realm," Rhistel explained. "I give my word it's a lot faster and safer," he eyed the boats once again— "than those vessels."

Ridge snorted and Rhistel appreciated at least one of them caught his humor. Not many did, now that he thought of it.

"Why don't you explain this portal to my men?" Ridge said. "It'll go down easier if they know what to expect."

Rhistel glanced around at the men and realized Ridge had made the right call. They all seemed more at ease with the suggestion.

"I've never had to explain the dynamics of a portal before, so bear with me. It's a gateway from one place to another, usually with the use of a token. In my case, Calista and I have a blood-link, which means wherever she is, I can pull up a portal to her location with only a sigil written in the air. May I?" Rhistel demonstrated the sigil, a glowing amber glyph he'd learned as a lad. "In other cases, if I've been to the location or can see it, I use a different glyph and the portal opens to it." Rhistel studied his surroundings. "Can I see this island from here?"

"That line of trees." Ridge pointed toward the horizon. "Do you see it?"

"That's where Zane is?"

"Yeah, is that good enough, or do you need to see it better?"

Rhistel canted his head at Ridge's question.

Cole searched in the bed of a nearby truck, picked out an object and brought it to Rhistel.

"Binoculars," Cole offered. "You can see the lay of the land better with these."

Cole quickly demonstrated how they worked and Rhistel took them, honing in on the wooded area.

"Thank you, this is what I needed." He handed the binoculars back to Cole. "Going through the portal is not harmful or disorienting, though the opaque substance is hard to describe. You'll understand once you go through. It's instantaneous, you walk through here and come out there." He pointed toward the island.

"If we're going to do this, let's get on with it," Ridge said. "I don't want to be searching for Zane at night. It's going to be bad enough if he doesn't want to be found, looking for a black wolf in the dark would be almost impossible."

Realizing the truth in his statement, Rhistel turned and studied the far-off island once again. Carefully sketching a glyph in the air, it immediately glowed and turned into an opening slightly taller than the men and about four feet wide.

"I'll hold it open for you. You have my word it's safe."

Ridge held his gaze for a time, and Rhistel knew his words were being weighed and he was being judged. The tall, black man called Reg strode past Ridge and through the portal. Before anyone said a word, the others followed, leaving Ridge and Rhistel alone.

"Your men are loyal and brave. It speaks volumes of your leadership," the fae observed.

"We're pack. We take care of each other. Anything happens to any one of them,"—Ridge's gaze was deadly—"and you will answer to me." Without another word, Ridge walked through the gateway.

Exhaling a breath and shaking his head, Rhistel muttered, "Duly noted" before he joined the shifters on the other side.

Ridge fought the urge to shake like a dog getting out of the water as he emerged from the fae's portal. It was as Rhistel had said. It had been quick, and he'd felt nothing, but it still gave him the frissons. Once this little excursion was over, he'd stick to walking, trucks, and boats, thank you very much. Apparently, the others felt the same way. They were a surly lot, but none the worse for wear when he checked on them.

"I figured I'd send the team out to track Zane while we check out the last resort, or do you want to handle it a different way?" Cole asked.

"Nah, sounds good. Make sure no one provokes him. Tell them to signal us and wait. I'd rather it be one of us who tries to bring him back. No sense in anyone getting hurt."

Ridge scanned the trees but knew it was a wasted effort. He wasn't going to spot Zane if his brother didn't want to be found. Ordinarily, it wouldn't have bothered him, but time wasn't on their side. He didn't talk about it, but he remembered—the pain, the loss, the grief—when he'd lost Heather, his Fated Mate. Only his brothers sticking to him like damn shadows had gotten him through it. With Zane's wolf not knowing if Callie was his mate, he was strictly in protective mode, not understanding the urgency of Zane having to come back.

Searching the ground away from the others, Ridge looked for any sign of tracks. He crouched beside a small bush, finding a couple of broken twigs and black hair lodged in the breaks. He'd had a hunch his brother would find comfort at the last resort, mostly because Callie's scent would be strongest there.

"Did you find something?" Rhistel asked.

Looking up, Ridge found the fae at his side, scouring the small island. He showed Rhistel the twigs and hair.

"He was here, not that it means anything. Cole and I are going to the last resort. I'd rather you stick with us. The enforcers are going to try to track Zane down. They'll signal if they find him."

"What is the last resort? I'm having difficulty finding a context for it," Rhistel admitted.

"Which serves the purpose. It's so outsiders don't know what we're talking about if they happen to overhear us, but it's called that because we go there when nothing else works."

"I see." Understanding dawned in Rhistel's eyes. "The last resort..."

"You'll see it soon enough. At first appearance, it's nothing more than an old abandoned cabin, but it's heavily warded from all supernatural entities. If you're inside, nothing is going to find you. Zane and Callie were staying there before the pendant was made for her. Unfortunately, it wasn't fail-proof."

"Calista told me about the pendant. She blames herself for losing it."

"None of this was her fault. She simply wanted to live her life. Your queen is to blame, if anyone is," Ridge vented.

"You're not wrong," Rhistel agreed. "I've tried to reason with her, but I'd get better results with that tree over there."

"I can only imagine." Ridge stopped at the edge of a small clearing. "There it is... the last resort."

"No offense, but it's not altogether what I expected."

"Exactly." Ridge grinned. "But wait, there's more." He winked at the fae and laughed out loud at the startled look on Rhistel's face.

Cole had slipped past them and opened the door without Rhistel seeing the camouflaged electronic keypad.

Rhistel's mouth literally dropped open after stepping inside.

"That never gets old." Cole barked a laugh.

"Wha—" Then the fae realized he'd been the brunt of the joke. Composing himself hastily, he flung back, "You have to admit it's a stark difference—the exterior, and... this." He waved his arms around.

"It was designed as such," Ridge agreed. "If someone should happen to wander onto the island, and it has happened a few times, no one would bother with the place. Going by the outside, it wouldn't shelter anything."

"Was magic involved in the construction?"

"Nah, only very talented carpenters. The only magic used was for the wardings, and Mancy checks on them regularly."

"I don't believe I've heard of this Mancy."

"Sorry about that," Cole interjected. "She was at the house with us, but she was doing some research, and none of us bother her when she's working."

Ridge totally agreed. "She's one female you don't want to get on the wrong side of."

"I remember seeing her. She had a unique tattoo on her face," Rhistel replied.

"Mancy is a member of the Ouma tribe. She received the facial tattoo when her father passed on all his healer teachings to her," Cole explained. "There are only a handful of the tribe who are shifters, and they choose to live here at Bayou Crescent. Merging their Native American heritage with their wolves was easier than most would think, but choosing between pack and tribe was a difficult choice. They have a strong tie to their tribe, too."

"She sounds fascinating. I would like to meet her one day if I may." Rhistel sounded thoughtful.

"We can introduce you after we get Callie back and things settle down. I'm sure she'll have a million questions for you. That female thirsts for knowledge. We're honored she's part of our pack," Ridge said solemnly.

The howl came from a distance, but Ridge and Cole turned as one toward the door.

"They found Zane," Ridge announced.

"I can sift, following you. I'll be right behind you," Rhistel said.

Ridge didn't bother to ask what he meant. They sprinted out the door. The next howl came seconds later, and Cole pointed to the northwestern part of the island.

"They're over there."

Ridge and Cole shifted, bounding through the trees.

Rhistel sifted ten... twenty feet at a time, always keeping the pair of wolves in sight. He needed to get to Zane. The message he carried was vital to the shifter's well-being, and Calista's life.

He was beginning to wonder exactly how big this 'tiny' island was when he saw the wolves ahead of them. Approaching the pack cautiously, he headed for Ridge, not wanting to agitate Zane more than he already was.

The black wolf was backed up against several trees growing close together while the enforcer team penned him in place. He growled and snarled, charging them, but never actually making a move against any of them. Ridge carefully approached his brother, speaking softly, his Cajun accent almost melodic in its cadence.

"Zane, I know you can hear me. Your wolf has done his job well, but we need you now. Callie needs you."

The black wolf whined at hearing Callie's name, shaking his head savagely. He took a step or two toward Ridge, then growled loudly, snapping at anyone who appeared to get too close. It was now or never, Rhistel needed this shifter whole again.

"Zane, I am Rhistel, blood kin of Calista. She sent me to find you. Nephinae has locked her away in the dungeons, surrounded by silver and iron. We need to get her out of there. Hear me, Zane. For the sake of your child, we need you!"

Time stood still as everyone stared at him in shock. Perhaps he should have warned them ahead of time, but he'd been too focused on reaching Zane.

The black wolf whined again, this time facing the fae. He canted his head, staring deep into Rhistel's eyes.

"It's true. I felt the life essence of the babe when I was with Calista. She loves you desperately and wants to be with you, to be a family."

The black wolf howled... long and mournfully, then haltingly began to shift. Rhistel winced as he watched the painful transformation. The others hadn't shifted like this, so it must have something to do with what Zane was going through that slowed his change. At long last, a man lay on the ground in the place of the wolf. He groaned as he struggled to sit up, looking over at Rhistel.

"Is it true? Callie carries my pup?"

"Yes, but the silver and iron are weakening her far too rapidly. I fear the child may not survive if we don't get to Calista soon."

"Tell me what I need to do."

Chapter 20

Zane adjusted the thigh sheath snugly against his leg. There was no way he was going into the fae realm without being loaded with iron, and fortune was on their side. They'd managed to dig up daggers with enough iron in them to get the job done. Zane wasn't planning on taking out the entire Sidhe court. He only wanted Callie back. Anyone who stood in his way would suffer the consequences.

If he'd had incentive before to go after Callie, it had doubled with the news she carried their child. They'd hadn't even gotten around to talking about family, though he knew without a doubt Callie was the only one for him, Fated Mate or not.

"Zane, I know you're in a hurry, but I wanted to let you know something before you left." Mancy approached him carrying two books, her finger marking a place in a third.

He tried to clamp down on his impatience. The healer was on his side, trying to help out as much as anyone else.

"What's up, Mancy?"

"I found what I need to break the curse on Callie's wolf." Mancy gave him a tight smile. "Bring her back, I can unbind the wolf."

Zane's breath hitched and tears burned his eyes. He pulled Mancy into his arms, hugging her tightly.

"Thank you, Mancy. I'll never be able to repay you for this."

"Bring her home, Zane."

With grim determination in his eyes, he stepped back.

"I'm going to do just that."

Zane mentally went over the plan one last time. It sounded easy enough, a simple snatch and grab. Rhistel would open the portal in the dungeon... they would eliminate the guards, get Callie and leave. He'd keep Callie at the last resort for now, and they'd deal with any fae repercussions later. Rhistel was planning on hanging around close to Callie for the time being, which was much appreciated protection.

He knew it wasn't fool-proof though, Zane needed something else—he needed to know the queen's weaknesses, if she had any. As desperate as he was to go charging in, he was smart enough to know they needed to have an edge.

"You ready, brother?" Ridge's voice was low, but it silenced the room.

Zane scanned the group before him—family, lifelong friends... pack. He trusted each of them with his life... and Callie's.

"Rhistel, this queen... Nephinae, does she have any weaknesses? Anything we can use to our advantage?"

Rhistel thought for a moment, his eyes widening as he looked Zane square in the eyes.

"How could I have forgotten? The princess! Nephinae has a daughter... Amantha. She's young, only thirteen summers. The queen is excessively protective of her. She keeps her away from the court most of the time."

"Does that mean she's not with the queen?" Zane asked.

"Oh, she's there," Rhistel explained. "Nephinae would never let the princess be beyond her reach, but she doesn't want the child to be influenced by the fae at court."

"I need her for insurance," Zane declared. Seeing the indecision on Rhistel's face, he went on hurriedly. "I'm not going to hurt her, I promise, but she's our ticket for safe passage."

"As long as you give your word, shifter. The child is innocent in all of this."

"As is mine." Zane glared at the fae.

"You're right. Forgive me." Rhistel thought for a moment. "If we don't attract undue attention, I can retrieve the princess while the rest of you subdue the guards."

"Sounds like a plan," Ridge announced. "Everyone ready?"

Zane's hurried glance found Mancy clearing off the dining table and laying out assorted items on a nearby counter. She must have felt Zane's gaze on her because she looked up and told him directly, "I'll be waiting for Callie. Be safe."

With a curt nod, he turned to Rhistel.

"Let's get Callie."

"Try again!"

Callie wiped the sweat from her brow and tried to focus on the object in front of her. She didn't understand what they wanted from her. The Master wanted her to use powers that had always been a hit-or-miss thing. She didn't know what she was capable of, and now she was weak and exhausted, not the best of conditions to work under.

Callie tried once more to focus. She'd moved things before, but it had always been under duress—like when she'd tossed that guy across the parking lot when she'd first started working at The Den.

Big mistake. The memory stirred up visions of Zane, and Callie stumbled.

"I said, Try again!" The lash slashed the back of her legs and she fell to her knees, the scream tearing from her lungs. Rough hands caught her arms, pulling her to her feet.

"It would be in your best interest to cooperate." The Master loomed in front of her. "The queen wants you in her service, though I have no idea why she'd bother with a hybrid in the first place," he sneered.

"If I could control my powers, you wouldn't be standing there, I promise," Callie choked out.

The slap whipped her head back against the guard holding her up, connecting with the armor and hard muscles beneath it. Callie groaned, her head throbbing and vision blurring.

"It's going to take more than that to best me, hybrid. The sooner you realize it, the better off you'll be." The Master stalked off, placing the whip on a rack holding assorted implements of torture. "Put her back in the cage. The queen wants to see her before we return her to the dungeon."

Tossing her into the cage, which wasn't much more than a large dog kennel, Callie crashed against the metal bars, the combination of silver and iron burning her flesh and leaving her crying out in pain. It was all she could do to crawl into a ball in the middle of the cage, trying not to touch any of the bars.

She cradled her stomach, clinging to the only joy left to her. Rhistel told her she was pregnant before he'd left to find Zane. Callie hadn't even realized it herself, but she didn't doubt the fae. Rhistel had told her about sensing a life essence once long ago in a conversation they'd had about her mother. She'd been gifted with the power, as had her brother. Usually, those with the gift went on to become healers but not all. Her mother and Rhistel had been exceptions.

Lying in a fetal position, Callie tried to rest while waiting for the appearance of Queen Nephinae. She prayed Rhistel and Zane would find a way to get her out of here. That small hope, and Zane's child, kept her fighting to hang on.

Zane and Cole entered the dungeon with the stealth and finesse of trained ninjas. Rhistel had opened the portal in an area away from where the guards congregated, giving them time to regroup before taking on the guards.

The dungeon was empty as far as Zane could tell. As the others joined them, they spread out, searching the cells, cautiously making their way to the main hall. Zane gave Rhistel a questioning look, who shrugged in answer. That wasn't any help. Where was Callie? What had they done with her? *What now?*

"Stay here. I'm going to see if I can find Callie, then the princess. Don't leave the dungeons."

With a short wave showing he understood, Zane moved to Ridge and Cole, sharing Rhistel's message. Waiting wasn't going to be easy. He needed to *do* something. Zane and his brothers were the ones in charge, not the ones taking orders. He had to remind himself it was for Callie's safety. They were in unknown territory and dependent on Rhistel to get them here and get them back home in one piece. It was a hard pill to swallow, but for Callie, he'd do anything.

"We have a situation," Rhistel whispered, as he crouched in front of them.

Zane was getting used to the abrupt appearances and disappearances of the fae. He was even a little envious of the sift power, not that he'd ever admit it.

"What are we dealing with?" Ridge asked.

"Calista is locked in a cage in the throne room. Nephinae and the Masters are gathering together now."

"Who and what are the Masters?" Zane asked.

"Long ago, the queen and I handpicked five men who are the best in all types of fighting skills and weaponry. They train all the soldiers under my command, so they aren't to be taken lightly. The queen calls them the Masters, and now, it's the only way they are referred to."

"What are they planning on doing to Callie?" Zane demanded.

"They're here to show Calista's skills to the queen. In her weakened state, I don't see how she can do what they ask of her. This won't go well."

"How many people are in the throne room?" Ridge pushed his long hair from his face in frustration. "There are only seven of us. We can't take on a roomful of guards and these Masters."

"That part is in our favor," Rhistel assured the alpha. "Nephinae likes these showings to be private. The guards will be excused from throne room until called to transport Calista back."

"It might be better to wait until Callie comes back here," Cole suggested. "We'd have a better chance with only a few guards."

"True, but I need this queen to realize we mean business. That won't happen unless we face her."

"I'm not crazy about it, but Zane is right," Ridge said. We can't have the fae chasing us back home. We need to get Callie and make sure the queen leaves us alone... for good."

"What about the princess?" Zane asked. "Where is she?"

"She was being dressed by her maid, and I overheard them speaking. Nephinae wants Amantha in the throne room with her."

"So much the better, everyone in the same place," Zane grunted in satisfaction.

"Keep in mind about the Masters. They won't be easy to overpower or subdue," Rhistel reminded the group.

"That's why we need to get Callie and outmaneuver the queen as fast as possible," Ridge stressed. "Cole and I will focus on releasing Callie while Zane and Rhistel will deal with the princess and the queen. Bixby, Steve, and Reg will distract the Masters long enough for us to get our parts done, then we're out. Agreed?"

Everyone rumbled in assent and stood, waiting for Rhistel to lead. Another portal, and it was game on.

Zane's gaze fell on Callie as soon as he cleared the portal. Forcing himself to turn away from her was one of the hardest things he'd ever done. He had to trust his brothers to care for her while he dealt with the queen.

A young girl was pushed into Zane's arms, and he held her arms fast.

"I won't hurt you, but the female in the cage is mine, and I mean to bring her home. The queen has to let her go. Do you understand?" Zane murmured into her ear.

"I do." The princess' gaze locked on her mother. She showed no fear nor made any effort to break free. Zane was impressed, the girl was brave beyond her years.

"Nephinae, Queen of the Sidhe court, I am Zane Landry and I've come for Calista Evans, my mate. If you try to stop us, I will take your daughter, as well. Leave us in peace, and we'll leave the same way."

"You wouldn't dare," the queen snarled. "You'll never make it out of this castle alive, and your little hybrid mate," she spat out the words, "will be the first to die."

"Let them go, Nephinae," Rhistel demanded. "What has your hatred for shifters gotten you?

Calista will never serve you. Haven't you taken enough from her? You killed her mother... my sister, my only family in this realm. You bound Calista's wolf, so she isn't even whole! What more could you possibly want? To what end? What have I ever done to you to deserve such treatment of the only family I have left?"

Zane took in the chaos exploding in the throne room. Bixby, Steve, and Reg were locked in battle with all five of the Masters, not giving any of them the opportunity to interfere with him or Ridge and Cole. He saw Ridge reach into the cage and gently lift Callie out and for the first time since she'd been taken, he was able to breathe.

"You fool! This is about so much more than those mangy shifters. Open your eyes! I would have given you everything, Rhistel. You could have ruled by my side, but you never gave me the attention I desired... the attention that should have been mine, your queen! Taking your family out of the picture, you should have turned to me, but still you fought me."

Rhistel looked as startled as Zane felt upon hearing Nephinae's declaration. Is that what this had been about the whole time—unrequited love... or a twisted version of it.

"I am leaving this court, Nephinae, and I'm taking my niece and her mate with me. Do not follow us and do not think to come after us at any point. Rule your realm and leave us in peace."

Rhistel opened a portal, openly glaring at the queen, daring her to make any kind of move.

A familiar snarl filled the room and Zane whirled around to see Ridge and Cole battling one of the Masters, while another was dragging Callie away. Zane swore. If he released the girl, he'd have no leverage with Nephinae, but there was no way in hell he was going to lose Callie.

"Go. I will attempt to reason with my mother."

Once again, the princess surprised Zane. Any other time or place, he would have been curious to know her story, but he had more pressing matters to deal with.

Shifting in mid-air, Zane launched himself upon the Master, knocking Callie free. She fell to the floor in a heap and Zane prayed she was all right. Locking his jaws on the back of the Master's neck, Zane struggled to maintain dominance, but the man was powerful and well-trained. With unheard of strength, the man grabbed Zane's leg and threw him across the room. Zane crashed into a wall, yelping in pain. Stone barriers didn't give easily, and he would feel the effects for days to come.

Shaking his head to clear the stars, he forced himself to get up. Once again, he sailed through the air to attack the Master, seconds before the man could get a hold of Callie. She still lay unconscious and Zane's heart beat erratically in his chest. She *had* to be all right.

Channeling every ounce of strength and energy he had left, Zane focused on the Master. Using teeth and claws, he tore and ripped, snarling his rage as blood flew in all directions. It was more than a few minutes before Zane realized that the man lay lifeless on the floor.

With a howl of triumph and fury, he rushed to Callie's side. Shifting, he felt for her pulse. With a sigh of relief, he found it, faint, but it was there.

"Get your woman, brother. It's time to leave."

Zane looked up at Ridge, who was just as covered in blood as he was. Gathering Callie tenderly in his arms, he glanced around the throne room. The five Masters were all dead, and the princess was speaking intensely to the queen as Rhistel watched the pair closely. Cole and his enforcers formed a circle around Zane.

Ridge, Cole, and the enforcers made a beeline for the portal. Zane held Callie tightly against his chest, looking at the queen, then Rhistel.

"Go, shifter," Nephinae spat. "It seems you have a champion in my daughter. I give you my word I will not enter your realm and I will leave you and the hybrid in peace." She turned to Rhistel, glaring at the fae. "Leave my court, and never return. I do this for Amantha, but I do it only once. Show your face again and I promise you, I will not be so lenient."

Zane caught the gaze of the princess and nodded to her. He wouldn't have a chance to thank her properly. By her smile, he knew she understood. Rhistel gestured for Zane to go through the portal and he didn't hesitate. He had no plans to ever enter this realm again.

Chapter 21

Callie slowly opened her eyes, not sure if she was dreaming. Soft sheets caressed her skin and a warm, comforting weight nestled beside her. Zane's soft snores reassured her that she was home... and safe. She caressed his cheek lightly, soaking in the sight of him. Zane's short hair was mussed, beard stubble was scratchy on her palm, and he'd never looked so handsome as he did right now.

"Hey gorgeous, did I wake you? Mancy fussed at me, but I had to be close to you."

Callie shook her head, too overcome with emotion to sort words into any semblance of sense.

Zane kissed her lightly on the lips, and before he pulled back, Callie wrapped her arms around him, deepening the kiss. He tasted of whiskey and outdoors, and she wanted him more than ever.

"Make love to me, Zane," she breathed into his mouth.

"I don't want to hurt you. You've had a rough go of it."

"Which is why I need you."

Zane didn't question her after that. Tenderly and with the gentlest of touches, he made love to her, unhurriedly and thoroughly. She cried out when she orgasmed, and Zane followed in her wake.

They lay together, wrapped in each other's arms, enjoying the peaceful moment and being together again. Callie's hand brushed against her stomach and the rush of memories flooded through her.

"The baby? Am I...?"

"The baby is still there," Zane assured her. "He's mine. He's going to be tough."

"What if it's a girl?" Callie asked coyly.

"She'll be tough, too, but she'll be my princess."

"Zane, I didn't know..."

"Shh, Rhistel explained it to me. You're still in the early stages. I can barely sense the pup myself."

"You're okay with it? I mean... what if we're not Fated Mates?" Callie bit her bottom lip. She loved Zane so much, she didn't think she could bear it if he turned away from her.

"Do you truly think we're not? You're my world Callie, you and our pup. Nothing can change my mind about how I feel for you. I love you, and I always will."

Zane wiped the tear from Callie's cheek with the pad of his thumb.

"I'm going to get Mancy so she can check you over. Once she says you're good to go, we're heading to the last resort. The full moon is tomorrow, and she found the ritual to unbind your wolf." He kissed the tip of her nose. "Before you start worrying... shifting will not hurt the pup."

Callie gave him a grateful smile. Zane always seemed to know how she was feeling or thinking, and she loved him even more for it.

"Give me a couple of minutes to clean up before you send her in," Callie said as she wrapped the sheet around her and headed to the bathroom.

"You got it, gorgeous."

Gorgeous. Every time Zane called her that, her heart fluttered. He made her *feel* gorgeous, which was a first for her. Everything about Zane was a first for her, and she treasured each moment with him.

A few minutes later Callie heard a light rap at the door, then it opened.

"Callie? It's Mancy. Zane said it was all right for me to come in."

Tossing her brush into the drawer, she met the healer in the bedroom.

"You must be feeling better." Mancy beamed at her. "At least you're moving on your own, which is a big improvement."

"It is," Callie agreed. "And I have you to thank for a lot of it. I didn't realize how much pain I was in from the iron and silver until you started treating the burns."

"The burns were severe, but the energy they were draining from you was the most dangerous part. The combination of the two metals was lethal. I'm not sure if the fae realized it." Mancy held out a small jar. "I'd like to treat those lashes on the back of your legs. Until we can get you shifting, healing is going to be a lot slower, and I don't want those marks to scar."

"I didn't even think about that." Callie stretched out on her stomach on the bed, and

Mancy began applying the ointment. "Zane told me you can break the curse on my wolf. Is it true?"

"Yes. It took some searching, but I found the ritual I'd been looking for. It's not overly complicated, just takes getting everything aligned at the right time. Hopefully, tomorrow evening you'll be shifting and joining us on the full moon run."

The pillowcase dampened as Callie's tears fell. To be able to shift and join a pack for a full moon run... she couldn't honestly remember the last one, it had been so long ago. This time, Zane would be with her, and they could run together, their wolves... Callie choked on a sob and Mancy comforted her as she gave into the emotions washing over her. The healer understood, and Callie was grateful for not having to explain those feelings threatening to break her.

Rhistel had offered the portal for Zane and Callie to get to the island, but Zane was secretly relieved when Callie sweetly thanked him, opting for the boat instead. There was nothing wrong with using the gateway, and Zane admitted it had its uses, but there were times when the simple things worked just as well and meant a bit more. Taking the boat over with Callie gave them more time to be with each other and added to his memories of the first time he'd taken Callie for a boat ride. Those were special times locked away in his heart, and he wanted to keep them there, adding more over the years.

Zane was counting the hours until tomorrow evening when Mancy would perform the ritual to unbind Callie's wolf. They would know then, without a doubt, whether they were Fated Mates. Not that it mattered either way to Zane... not at this point. Callie was as much a part of him as any mate could be, Fated or not. Either way the ritual went, Zane was claiming her under the full moon tomorrow night, and she would officially be his mate.

After tying off the boat, Zane and Callie adjusted their backpacks filled with the few supplies they'd brought, then, hand-in-hand, they headed for the sanctuary of the last resort. They'd gone only a small distance when Callie stopped short.

"What's wrong?"

"What if they come after us?"

"They won't. Rhistel's keeping watch over the situation."

"He's back at your place. How is that keeping watch?" Callie persisted.

Zane faced her, a hand on each slim shoulder. He could feel her tremble under his fingers and knew how deep her fear ran.

"I spoke with your uncle before we left. He has trusted allies at court who will be his eyes and ears. If need be, he can be here in an instant." Zane pulled her into his arms, holding her tightly. "Once we're in the cabin, nothing can touch us," he breathed against her ear. "Take a breath, gorgeous. We'll be there in five minutes."

She looked up at him, and his heart tightened. She trusted him. He would die before he broke that trust.

Callie jerked her head quickly. "Okay, let's do this."

Taking her hand again, they jogged the rest of the way. Zane saw the relief in Callie's eyes when he keyed in the code to unlock the door. He didn't say anything about the long exhalation of breath she probably didn't even realize she'd let loose. They'd made it, and she felt safe. It was all that mattered. Zane had no plans of leaving the cabin until Mancy and Ridge came for them the next evening.

"I don't want to bring up bad memories, but something has been on my mind," Zane started.

"What do you mean?" Callie asked.

"The pendant. The girls found it in one of your bags. Did you take it off?"

"No!" Callie's hand automatically went to the spot where the pendant would have laid against her chest. "I... I really don't know, unless it came off when I was changing clothes in the dressing room. My bags were on the floor around me, it could have dropped into one of them."

"That makes sense." Zane looked thoughtful. He glanced at Callie and recognized the anxiety rising once again. "Hey, it's over. I'm sorry I brought it up. I just wondered about it."

"I'm sorry I was so careless."

Zane captured her hands and kissed each fingertip.

"You were not careless. It was an accident, one we'll put behind us."

Stowing their backpacks on the counter, Callie looked around the cabin.

"What do you want to do?"

The growl was out before he could suppress it and Callie giggled.

"I'm a guy, did you expect different?" He felt like a Neanderthal, but some things couldn't be helped.

"No, and just so you know... I wouldn't change a thing." Callie walked into his arms and nipped his bottom lip.

"Damn good thing." He inhaled her essence and felt himself go rock hard. She felt so good... so right in his arms. This was the only time he felt whole anymore.

"How about we take this to the bedroom?" Callie gave him a come-hither look and fluttered long lashes at him, and damn if that didn't make him even harder.

Scooping her into his arms, Zane wasted no time in getting to the bedroom. He briefly thought of different positions to try all over the little cabin, but right then, he wanted the expanse of a king-sized bed to explore the beauty in his arms.

Her laugh was sensual and open, and his pulse quickened with desire. His fingers ached to touch her soft skin, his mouth to taste her. Callie scooted away from him and knelt in the middle of the big bed, watching him from under lowered lids as she unbuttoned her shirt. His breath caught as the glimpse of a full round breast came into view.

"You are so damn beautiful," he husked. Zane dropped his jeans to the floor and ripped off his t-shirt, letting it fly across the room. With a will he didn't know he possessed, he stayed in place, stroking himself as he watched Callie lazily divest herself of clothing, taunting him, making him want her desperately.

Animal hunger taking over, he stalked her, nuzzling the side of her neck, and inhaling her scent as his tongue tasted her flesh. She shuddered when he rasped the junction of her shoulder and neck. He felt his fangs elongate, the almost overwhelming urge to sink them deep into her neck, marking her—claiming her—but it wasn't the time. He wanted to claim her under the full moon, when his wolf would be the strongest. He knew in his heart she was his Fated Mate, but he also wanted his beast to acknowledge her as theirs.

Their lovemaking was intense, joined together by more than flesh, by their souls as well. Callie drove him wild and his hunger couldn't be denied. She aroused every sense, every thought in him, setting his soul on fire. The bed creaked beneath them as their passions flared to new heights. He demanded more from her, and she gave willingly and openly, loving him with a fierceness he'd never known from another.

Callie gasped with each measured thrust, sensations building fast and furious. Zane possessed her mouth as he teetered on the brink, then fell into impossible pleasure. His senses shattered when he came inside her, and her nails raked his back as she cried out his name.

Sated, he fell back onto the bed, cradling Callie in his arms. Zane's sleep was dreamless and deep.

Chapter 22

Callie snuggled against Zane's warmth, his arms encircling her even in his sleep. She felt safe, loved, and cherished—three words that usually didn't apply to her, but now meant the world.

So much was banking on tonight, Callie didn't know how she would get through the day. If ever there was a way to make time fly, she wanted it now.

"You are way too serious too early in the morning," Zane grumbled against her ear. "I demand either coffee or morning love before you throw anything at me."

"Coffee sounds good, now that you mention it." Callie winked at him, pulling the sheet back.

"Coffee can wait," he growled. "Get back in here."

Callie laughed, loving his growl, his possessiveness—then she saw the heat in his eyes, and she melted. He was right... coffee and the world could wait.

She took back her earlier thought of wanting to speed through the day. Instead, the thought of more days like this one was heading the top of her list. It seemed anything involving Zane guaranteed a special place in her heart.

"It won't be long before Mancy and Ridge get here. You ready for this?" Zane let the curtain fall back over the window as he turned to her, coffee mug in one hand, nothing but low-riding jeans hugging his slim hips.

"As ready as I'll ever be, I guess." She crossed the room to stand in front of him, taking the mug from his hand and setting it down. Callie wanted no distractions. She touched his lips with a playful finger which was immediately sucked into his mouth. She moaned at the sensation, knowing full well the advantage was in his court because she was now putty at his feet. His lips crushed against hers, the kiss hot and wet with desire. Zane tugged at her shirt when a knock sounded on the door.

"Fuck, my brother has the absolute worst timing," Zane grumbled as he tried to straighten Callie's shirt, only making things worse.

"It's on me. I started it, knowing we didn't have the time." She giggled, slapping his hands away.

"Believe me, we'll finish this later," Zane growled.

"I have no doubt." Callie laughed gaily as she swung the door open to find Mancy looking uncomfortable, Ridge, a bit on the sheepish side, and Cole, openly enjoying himself. *Damn enhanced shifter senses.* There were no secrets within a hundred yards of these guys.

"Sorry about the interruption, but Mancy wanted to set up for this evening and go over the ritual with you," Ridge explained.

"Not a problem," Callie said brightly.

"Speak for yourself," Zane grumbled.

"I think that's what she did," Cole smirked.

Mancy gestured to Callie to walk outside with her.

"We'll leave them alone for a while. I'm sure Ridge wants to go over preparations for the run tonight." Mancy led Callie to the back of the cabin to a small, cleared area with a firepit about twenty feet away.

"What kind of preparation does the pack need for a run? My old pack literally shifted and ran," Callie said.

"It's not so much the run, but officially welcoming you to the pack and announcing you and Zane as mates."

"Everyone is so sure we're mates." Callie worried. "I love Zane, don't get me wrong, but this whole Fated Mate thing has me stressed. What if we're not, Mancy?"

Mancy stopped what she was doing and turned to Callie.

"Anyone can look at the two of you and know you're mates. I've never seen two people more destined to be together." Mancy gave her an encouraging smile. "Have you spoken to Zane about your fears?"

"I have, and he said it didn't matter to him, one way or the other, but deep down, it has to matter. He's pack, he's the Beta... why would he want to mate with anyone who wasn't his Fated Mate?"

"Calista Evans, if you truly think that, then you don't know Zane Landry. If that male says he loves you, then that's it, case closed. Let me tell you something about him. I watched him grow up and become the man he is today. He has *never* fallen in love before meeting you. Oh, sure, there have been females, but nothing serious."

"He's not a flirt like Cole, honey. Zane always treated his lovers with discretion and respect, but they knew they weren't his Fated Mate, and that's what Zane has been holding out for. Here he is now, head over heels in love with you, and you think y'all aren't Fated? I wouldn't even give it a thought."

"I hope you're right." Callie worriedly bit her bottom lip.

"We'll know soon enough." Mancy smiled warmly. "Now, come over here and help me get set up."

Zane cracked his knuckles and gave a worried look toward the door Callie and Mancy had just walked out of.

"What's on your mind, Zane?"

Ridge's low voice cut through the press of worry and doubt racing through Zane's head.

"Everything, I guess."

"Bro, you got this." Cole gave him a reassuring squeeze on the shoulder. "There is no way she's not your Fated Mate. In another hour, y'all are gonna be running through the trees with the rest of us."

"Yeah, you're right." Zane tried to shake off the case of nerves that had settled like a cloak around his shoulders. It was probably Callie's doubts rubbing off on him. He had this. He *had* to have this.

"Go on with Mancy and Callie." Ridge gestured toward the door. "Cole and I are going to stay in here for the ritual."

Zane stared at his brothers for a moment, memories of them always being there for him, for each other, and tonight was no different.

"Thanks, for everything." He walked out the door.

Approaching the clearing, Zane saw Mancy helping Callie put on a simple white gown. She gave him a tremulous smile as he got closer and had to fight the urge to take her into his arms. He wanted to hold her, to touch her, but for now, it had to wait.

"Everything set up?" Zane asked.

"Yes," Mancy replied. "We were waiting on you to start."

Callie gracefully knelt in front of the firepit and waited for Mancy. Zane glanced at the healer, and she gestured toward Callie. With a deep breath, he walked over to the small fire and knelt across from Callie.

Mancy knelt between them and began adding herbs to the fire, making it hiss and crackle, as she chanted low in a language Zane had never heard before. When she reached for Callie's hand, she pulled out a dagger and swiftly sliced her palm, letting the blood flow into the fire. The flames leapt higher, and Mancy's chanting grew faster. Blue and green smoke billowed out of the pit until they were surrounded, not able to see through it, barely able to see each other.

Callie groaned and Zane worriedly peered through the smoke, but Mancy's hand on his arm kept him in place. Callie fell to her side and began to thrash about wildly. Zane turned panic-stricken eyes to the healer, but with a look, she assured him it was part of the ritual. He knew better than to speak or break Mancy's concentration. Any little distraction could ruin the ceremony, and that was the last thing he wanted.

After what felt like forever, Callie calmed, lying quietly on the ground. Mancy sat back, letting out a low groan.

"That was intense," Mancy observed. "Now we wait."

"Wait for what?" Zane wanted to know.

"For Callie to wake and see if her wolf is with her."

"How long will that take?"

Mancy gave him a side-eye and smirked.

"Like I do this every day?" She barked a laugh. "She'll wake when she's ready."

"Great. More waiting." Zane grumbled.

"What else do you have to do?" Mancy asked.

"I'm sorry, I guess I'm more nervous than I realized."

"I'm messing with you, Zane. Callie is fine. Her wolf needs to find her way back. It may take a while."

The sound of boats approaching filled the air, followed by laughter and easy conversation of the pack as they made their way onto the island for the night's run. Zane glanced at Callie, who still slept quietly on the ground before him. Mancy passed him a bottle of water, which he took gratefully. As he swallowed the last of the cooling liquid, he saw Callie move out of the corner of his eye. Tossing the empty bottle, he motioned to Mancy.

"She's waking up."

Groggy at first, Callie looked around until she saw Zane.

"Is it over? What happened?"

Zane helped her to sit up.

"The ritual is over. The rest is on you and your wolf. How do you feel?"

Callie fell silent, her gaze cast toward the ground. After a few moments, she looked up.

"I feel the same as before. Does this mean it didn't work?" Fear shone in her eyes as she searched for Mancy.

"It means nothing of the sort, child," Mancy assured her calmly. "Search for her, call to her." Mancy turned to Zane. "I want your wolf to call to her. Can you do that?"

"I can try."

"I'm going inside to talk to Ridge. I want you both to try to get your wolves to connect. Let the magic happen, don't fight it."

"Just like that, huh?" Callie said softly.

"It's worth a shot, gorgeous. We've come too far to quit now."

Sitting cross-legged in front of Callie, holding hands, Zane called his wolf from the void. It didn't take a second. It seemed his beast had been on the edge and watching the whole time. He tried to explain what he needed from his wolf, then waited.

Zane's black wolf howled, low, long, and mournful, then again, this time louder and more forceful. Zane's heart filled with hope and longing. She had to answer, she simply had to!

Callie's hands tightened around his and she gasped.

"I feel her."

"Can you bring her out from the void?"

"She's... she's coming. Zane, I see her!" Tears streamed down Callie's cheeks.

Zane once again called upon his wolf to call Callie's beast. He swallowed hard. His wolf was up front and standing, staring straight at Callie—his howl demanding.

"She's so beautiful," Callie breathed. "I'd forgotten how beautiful she was."

Mate.

"Yes!" Zane shouted. They laughed and cried in each other's arms as their wolves danced about, tails wagging as they proclaimed finding their mate.

Zane's mouth crushed Callie's lips, claiming her with a savage kiss. Any vestige of doubt was erased, eradicated by the sanction of their wolves. Fated Mates.

"Can you shift?" Zane asked, tugging on Callie's hands.

Callie stood before Zane, and with a tug, the gown pooled at her feet. In an instant, a glossy chestnut wolf with chocolate-colored eyes stood before him. Zane had never seen anything more beautiful in his life.

Shifting to his wolf, he howled his joy and together, they bounded off into the woods.

Hours later, Zane and Callie returned to the cabin. They would spend one last night here, returning home in the morning. For now, they had a house guest, and while Zane had no problem with Rhistel living with them, he wanted to spend this night alone with Callie.

Zane scooped Callie into his arms, carefully depositing her onto the bed. He felt like he'd been waiting for this forever, and there was nothing that could stop him from claiming his mate.

Callie pulled him into her arms, and they made love slow and tenderly. As passions flared, fueled by hunger, Zane moved hard and fast, the need to explode building to a wild crescendo. Rolling Callie to her knees, he entered her from behind, clasping her hips and pulling her hard into his final thrust. He growled with pleasure as he spilled inside her, fangs sinking deep into her shoulder at the same time. His wolf howled triumphantly as they claimed their Fated Mate. Callie was finally his.

A while later, coming out of the bathroom, Zane found Callie sitting in the middle of the bed, fiddling with a small box in her hands.

Tossing the towel into a hamper, Zane looked at her curiously.

"What do you have there?"

"Kitty brought it to me. I'd asked her to hold it for me, but she figured I might want to give it to you tonight instead."

Zane sat down beside her.

"What is it?"

"An early birthday present." Callie smiled, then it faltered. "I didn't think I would be here for your birthday. That's why I gave it to Kitty. Even if we weren't together, I wanted you to have it."

She held the box out to him.

Taking it carefully from her fingers, he opened the small container and saw the cross.

"It's beautiful."

"Turn it over."

The engraved crescent moon was intricate and well done, but the wording was what did him in.

"I don't know what to say, Callie. It's perfect."

"I was hoping you'd like it." She beamed at him. "Kitty said she took it upon herself and had Mancy magically alter the chain. She said it will adjust to you whether you're in human or wolf form. That way, you can't lose it."

He wasted no time in putting the cross around his neck.

"I'll never take it off."

Callie's eyes glistened with unshed tears.

Pulling her into his arms, Zane kissed her slow and thoroughly, deep and passionately. She was his world, his everything, his Fated Mate, and soon, the mother of his pup. He was the luckiest of males. He had everything a man could hope for.

The Bayou Crescent Wolves
continues in book two...

Cole

Cole
Bayou Crescent Wolves,
Book Two

The world is Cole Landry's oyster. As Enforcer of the Bayou Crescent wolfpack, he lets his older brothers handle the details of pack life while he keeps everyone in line. Theirs is a laid-back lifestyle so, no stress, right? It gives him time to love the ladies, what Cole does best... until he meets the one female he can't charm.

Fox shifter, Kenzie Butler is done with men. Cheated on too many times, she's tired of having her heart broken. She's better off alone, focusing on herself to heal. When an old friend invites her to spend Christmas in a small Louisiana town, Kenzie jumps at the chance. This could be the healing haven she's searching for... until she meets an annoying, egocentric wolf shifter who always seems to show up wherever she is.

When Kenzie's ex shows up in Bayou Crescent to claim her, Cole has to own up to his true feelings for the standoffish little vixen or lose her forever.

Before You Go!

If you liked this book, please do me a huge favor and leave a review. Reviews are a small thing that mean so much to authors. They're invaluable as a means of advertising.

Thanks in advance!

Madison Granger
AUTHOR

Also, By Madison Granger

Paranormal Romance

The Kindred Series
Phoenix Rising
Eternal Embrace
A Destiny Denied
Blindsided
Deuces Wild
Fated Journey
A Warrior's Redemption

The Amelia Series
The Awakening of Amelia
The Rising of Amelia

Stand-Alone
Save The Last Dance
Heart of Stone
A Valkyrie's Vow
Gambit
An Unexpected Legacy
Claiming Magick

Urban Fantasy

To Kill a Demon

PHOENIX RISING

Book One of The Kindred Series

———————

Madison Granger

CHAPTER 1

Torie conceded to two thoughts simultaneously...
Christmas shopping was overrated, and the spirit
of Christmas was dead, buried under a glittering
blanket of commercialism. She'd never been a big
fan of crowds. There were way too many people
out and about this weekend for her liking. She was
doing her best to forge through the masses to get
the last elusive gift items on her list. Then there
was the traffic. *Seriously! Does everyone think they
have the only vehicle on the road?* It seemed the
streaming multitude left their IQ's and common

sense at home. If she made it to her house in one piece, she would consider herself a holiday shopper survivor.

Torie parked her SUV, sighing with resignation about the things she couldn't control. Grabbing her cell phone, keys, and purse, she headed across the full parking lot to the local bookstore. She'd been out all morning and most of the afternoon in search of Christmas presents for friends. Usually, she shopped online, but sometimes you just had to get out and fight the crowds for that *perfect* gift. Unfortunately, those *perfect* gifts were getting harder and harder to find, or someone else had the same idea and by the time Torie got to the shelf, they were already gone. Frustration was rearing its ugly head. She'd come to the realization that she needed an indulgence break before continuing her search. A book for herself and a shot of caffeine should brace her for the rest of the shopping day.

Entering The Literal Word, she was regaled with bright lights, colorful displays, and Christmas music playing over the speakers. Torie loved this store. She delighted in the convenience of shopping online, but there was nothing like browsing aisles and shelves of books.

Here, she was in her element. Books were her comfort zone, friend, and solace when she needed mental pampering. As she glanced around the setup, Torie took in the crowd browsing for books or the latest book-related gadget, and there were plenty of them. People were running into each other trying to get through narrow passages to look at all the items.

Java Joe's, the in-house coffee shop, was also catering to a maximum crowd. Wistfully, Torie wondered if she would be able to get a cappuccino after she'd made her purchases. Slinging her bag up on her shoulder, she navigated to her favorite section. A romance book with a sexy werewolf or vampire was always a welcome escape from her busy, but lonely life. An auburn-haired, green-eyed middle-age divorcee, Torie was a graduate of the *been there, done that, have a drawer full of t-shirts* school of life. After more than her share of failed relationships, she was pretty sure the rest of her life was going to be spent alone. Being on the more-than-curvy side insured it. Men her age seemed to all want that pretty, young trophy-type on their arm. *It is what it is* had become her mantra.

It wasn't a bad life, in itself. Torie had family, a brother and sister. She also had a grown daughter and a precocious granddaughter she adored. She had a job she liked, and made a decent living, too. There just wasn't a special man in her life. That kind of loneliness was hard for her. It had been a long time since there had been anyone memorable. Torie missed the best parts of a relationship, the companionship, sharing of ideas and thoughts, laughter, and the sex. *Yeah, I miss the sex.* Shaking her head ruefully, she berated herself for the pity party. That kind of thinking was depressing and never got her anywhere. It was time to shove it back into that tiny compartment in her brain and try, once again, to forget about it.

Approaching the paranormal romance section, Torie noticed they'd added a tier of shelves right before it of new releases. *Well, this makes it a little easier to find what I'm looking for.* Browsing through the titles, she scanned for releases by her favorite authors first. Torie picked up a few unknowns and started reading the back covers to find her next book boyfriend. After selecting a couple that seemed promising, she ambled over to another section of her favored genres, science fantasy. There was one book that had been released recently. She wondered if it was on the shelf yet, or if she would have to order it.

When she got to the section, Torie spotted her goal on a lower shelf. *Naturally! Why do they have to put them way down there?* Bending down, she grabbed the book. As she straightened, she lost her balance, dropping books and purse with a crash. Reddening with embarrassment, Torie bent down to retrieve her goods with a muttered oath. A man's strong, long-fingered hand came into her line of vision, reaching for her books as Torie grabbed her purse.

"Allow me," entreated an amused deep voice. He held her arm, lending her his support so she could stand.

Flustered beyond belief, still blushing furiously, Torie peered up to thank the man for his kindness. She gazed into the most mesmerizing pair of sky-blue eyes she'd ever seen. Torie found herself struck dumb. She took in his shaved head, and a handsome face with a sexy soul patch under his bottom lip, and a drop-dead killer smile.

"Tha... thank you." She finally managed to stammer.

"Always a pleasure to assist a lady in distress." He smiled back at her.

The handsome stranger held the books out to her. Regaining her composure, Torie reached up to take them. She couldn't help but notice how very tall he was. She looked up to give him a grateful smile. His tailored slacks and button-down shirt did nothing to disguise the definition of a well-sculpted body. The rolled sleeves partially covered what appeared to be a full sleeve of tribal tattoos on his right arm. *Oh my, this guy is the stuff fantasies are made of.*

His gaze went from her arms loaded with books to making eye contact.

"Have you found everything you were looking for?"

His smile, devastatingly sexy, sent her heart into overdrive. It'd been ages since she found herself attracted to any man, and here was her proverbial *sex on a stick,* talking to *her.* She said a quick prayer not to flub this.

"Yes, as far as shopping for books goes, I'm pretty well done."

"In that case," he started, his voice low and husky, "could I interest you in a coffee?"

Torie swallowed hard. He seemed sincere. There was no way she was going to pass up the chance to find out who this gorgeous guy was. Her mouth curved into a smile.

"I'd love some coffee. Thanks. Let me pay for my books first, and I'll meet you there."

Sweeping an arm out toward the front of the store, he motioned for her to go first.

"I shall wait for you."

Throwing him a quick smile, she got in line, hoping it wouldn't take long to pay for her books. For once, there were enough employees behind the counters. Checkout went quickly and she met up with her good Samaritan.

"What kind of coffee would you like?"

Torie always got flustered trying to make decisions at coffee shops. There were so many to choose from and she never could decide what she wanted, unlike everyone else who rattled off complicated mixtures. The man asking the question now upped the ante. Looking up at the lighted sign on the wall, she noticed the highlighted special.

"The Spiced Gingerbread Cappuccino sounds interesting." She crossed her fingers in hopes that it was a decent choice.

Walking to the counter to place their orders, he turned back to her.

"Would you mind getting a table for us? I will be there shortly with our coffees."

As Torie glanced around the crowded room, her gaze locked on a table that was being vacated. She hurried over, cleaned up after the couple who'd left everything behind, and disposed of the trash. In the few minutes she had to wait for the handsome stranger to join her, she tried to regain her composure and get her act together. *She was acting like a schoolgirl, for crying out loud.* It had been such a long time since she had any social interaction with a man, she was sorely out of practice and nervous. As he neared the table, she once again marveled at him. He was drop-dead gorgeous. This stranger was everything she'd ever fantasized about when it came to the perfect man. Now she would find out if his personality matched the outside. She sighed. *A woman could only hope.*

He carefully placed their coffees on the table and sat across from her. The table and chairs weren't small, yet he seemed to dwarf everything around him. Not only was he a big man, but his presence seemed to add *more* to his already dominating size.

"My name is Quinn McGrath, and you are?" He introduced himself with a heart-melting smile.

Flustered by his sensuous smile, Torie bit her lip before returning the introduction.

"I'm Torie Masters. Thank you for the coffee... and again for your help earlier."

"Not a problem, believe me. I am glad I was in the right place at the right time."

To her relief, their conversation went smoothly. She'd never been very good at small talk. He kept the conversational flow going by asking questions and listening intently to her answers. Torie discovered that Quinn, like her, was an avid reader. He preferred mysteries and a little science fiction, having several favorite authors in both genres. From books, they ventured to movies and music. She was continually surprised at how much they had in common. The conversation between them flowed easily and the banter was light and casual, making the time pass quickly.

When Torie heard her phone chime with a text, she checked it hastily. She'd heard the faint chime a couple of times before but had ignored it. She'd been enjoying her conversation too much to want to be interrupted. Figuring her daughter was going to be persistent until she replied, she tapped out a quick answer. Looking at the clock on the face of her phone, she was astonished to find that more than two hours had passed. She noticed a slight look of disappointment flitting across Quinn's handsome face as she checked the messages.

"Do you have to go?"

"No, not at all. My daughter is checking on me. I'm not usually out this long," she confessed.

"Excellent. Could I persuade you to have dinner with me? I am enjoying your company and I really am not ready for our time together to end."

Torie's initial reaction was to thank him politely and decline the invitation, but she hesitated. Here was a super attractive man who seemed genuinely interested in her. They had spent the last two hours caught up in captivating conversation. *Why **not** have dinner with him? What could it possibly hurt?* It had been way too long since she'd enjoyed the company of a man. She was going to do this.

"I realize we do not know each other yet." Quinn must have understood her hesitancy. "There is a steak house right across the parking lot, we can walk over there to have dinner. You will not be far from your vehicle." He placed his hand over hers briefly. "Would that make you feel a little more secure?"

Didn't that just seal the deal?

"I would really like that. Thank you." She accepted his invitation with a gracious smile.

Quinn cleared away their coffee cups. Coming back to the table, he reached for her purchases.

"Would you like to put these in your vehicle before we go to the restaurant?"

"That would be great. My truck is right out front." Feeling like he was reading her mind, she readily agreed.

With a hand on the small of her back, Quinn escorted her out of the bookstore and to her SUV. She stashed her bag in the back with her other purchases before making sure it was locked. They walked through the still-full parking lot to Vincent's Restaurant. It was one of her favorite places to eat. The aroma of grilled steaks and freshly baked bread filled the air, greeting them before they reached the door.

Entering the dimly lit, crowded eatery threw Torie's assaulted senses into overload. The dining area echoed with laughter, music, plates clanging, and murmured conversations. Trying to acclimate to the soft lighting and not get crushed by the crowd was a challenge. Quinn took charge immediately, using his body to protect her from the hordes of people rushing around them. He put an arm around her shoulders, drawing her close. It was all Torie could do not to melt right into Quinn's side. *He's so very strong... and rock solid... and his scent... what was that? Sandalwood, sage, both? It was glorious, whatever it was.* She wanted to stay right where she was, drinking him in.

Quinn flashed a charming smile at the hostess, and they were quickly led to their seats. Torie wondered how it happened so fast, considering there was a group of people standing around the entrance, obviously on a wait list. She saw the young woman beaming up at Quinn, trying her best to be flirtatious. Torie smiled to herself. She couldn't blame the attendant for trying. If it got them a table, then more power to her and Quinn.

Pulling out a chair for her, Quinn waited until she settled in her seat before taking his own chair. He ran his hand lightly over Torie's shoulders as he walked by. *Brownie points for manners.* She indulged in an inward thrill at his touch, grateful she hadn't been wearing a jacket or coat that would have hampered the feel of his caress. As much as she enjoyed colder weather, the winters in southern Louisiana were usually mild.

"Is this to your liking?" Quinn asked, pulling her from her thoughts.

"Yes, it's fine," she replied, still amazed at how quickly they had been seated.

A server came up immediately to take their drink orders, leaving them for a few minutes to go over their menus, and make their choices. Finding out how akin their preferences were in other areas, it wasn't all that surprising to discover they had similar tastes in food and how it was prepared. The conversation quickly picked up where it had left off at the bookstore. She found out that he was a financial consultant and owned his own business, McGrath Consulting. His brother, who had a corporate law background, was his partner. Quinn was looking for office space in the New Orleans and surrounding areas which had led him to Torie's hometown.

Their conversation paused when the server returned with their meals. As the food was placed in front of them, Quinn assured the server that everything was fine, and the young man left them to enjoy their meal. Resuming their talk, Quinn questioned her about her job.

Torie was a little abashed to admit she was just a receptionist. He was quick to quash the *just* part of her job description. When he spoke to her, she felt like she was important, that what she did counted. Torie knew he was right. She did a lot more than simply answer phones and take messages, though seldom did anyone think of it that way, especially her boss.

Over their meal, Quinn regaled her with stories of his childhood in Scotland. Torie was fascinated. She'd always dreamed of visiting Scotland but didn't think she would ever get the chance to travel. He had a way of telling stories that took her there, making her visualize the lovely scenery and the antics of two young brothers growing up in the Highlands.

"I have to say, for growing up in Scotland you don't have much of an accent," she observed between bites.

"It is true. It has faded over time." Quinn nodded. "I have been away from Scotland for many years now. I have traveled the world over, several times. When you have had as many business dealings as I have with people of different cultures you tend to lose the accent.

"Dinna fash yirsel lassie. Ah kin pull it oot whin a'm needin' it." Aiming a disarming smile her way, he spoke in a thick Scottish brogue, capping it off by throwing her a roguish wink.

"Yes indeed, you can. It's still there." Torie laughed in delight.

Lingering over coffee after their meal, Torie glanced around the room. It dawned on her that only a few patrons remained.

"I guess we better call it a night. They'll be closing on us pretty soon."

"Time seems to have gotten away from me today." Quinn reluctantly agreed. "I will walk you back to your vehicle." They wound their way through the tables, to make their way outside. Taking her hand, Quinn escorted Torie back to her truck.

"Is there a chance I can see you tomorrow? I do not wish to rush you, but there is a reason for my asking."

"What do you mean?" Torie regarded him quizzically.

"I am going to be out of town for the next two weeks on business. I have really enjoyed my time with you today and I want to see you again before I have to leave," Quinn explained. "Please say yes."

"How can I possibly say no to that?" She smiled brightly.

"Excellent!" Quinn replied with a broad grin. "Lunch, then?"

"Lunch, it is." Laughing, Torie nodded.

After exchanging phone numbers, Torie got into her SUV. In her rearview mirror, she could see Quinn stand in place as he watched her drive off, then slowly walk to his own car.

Torie drove home in a daze. *Who knew that today would be the stuff dreams were made of?* Parking her truck under the carport, she heard the chime that let her know she had a text message. Glancing down at her cell phone, she saw it was from Quinn.

Thank you for today. I look forward to seeing you tomorrow. ~Q.

Hugging herself, she knew she was going to have the most pleasant of dreams that night.

AN UNEXPECTED LEGACY

———————

Madison Granger

Chapter 1

Rafe Martin ran his hands lovingly over the surface of the long, polished oak table. Weathered by age and use, it was still a thing of beauty in his eyes. He'd spent long hours making it, taking pleasure in every aspect of the process.

Now he sat at the head of the table, a bowl of steaming stew in front of him. Smelling the delicious aroma all day, he was eagerly awaiting dinner. He closed his eyes in bliss after taking a huge bite. Dottie could create a fantastic meal from the most meager supplies, but the woman excelled at her stew. It was his favorite, and his aunt knew it.

He heard the commotion long before they approached his cabin. Shaking his head in resignation, he hurriedly got in a few more bites before the inevitable knock on the door. Passing a napkin over his mouth, he downed half of his sweet tea, then opened the door just as the man was going to knock.

"What is it, Riley?"

"Sorry to disturb your dinner, Alpha, but we thought you'd want to see this."

Rafe looked past him to see two others carefully carrying an injured man. They laid him down gingerly on his front porch. Rafe sniffed the air. He was wolf; whoever had done this meant business. The man was in no condition to shift.

"He's going to need a healer. Call Miriam." Turning to Riley, he asked, "Who is he, and where did you find him?"

"Found him in a ditch up the road. Best we could tell, he got dumped. Hasn't been able to talk much, pretty sure his jaw's busted in a couple of places, but he managed to get out a name."

"I'm not going to like the answer, am I?" Rafe studied the injured man.

"Afraid not." Riley took a deep breath. "It was Tom Sanders."

Rafe crouched down in front of the injured man and gently moved his head from side to side, noting the extensive bruising and swelling. The stranger moaned.

"It's all right, fella. You're safe, and we're going to see to your injuries."

An older woman, wearing jeans and a loose t-shirt, with snow-white hair hanging loose around her shoulders, approached the cabin.

"I hear you have someone for me to tend. What are we looking at?" Miriam Baxter, pack healer, winced at the sight of the injured man.

"We have a mess, Miriam. He's gonna need a ton of help."

"I'll say." Turning to the growing crowd milling around the porch, Miriam picked out two. "Danny, run to my cabin and get the stretcher I keep in the shed. Then you and Steve can carry this fella to my guest room. Handle him with care, boys. He's messed up pretty bad." Miriam affectionately patted Rafe on the arm. "I'll let you know how he's doing."

"Thanks, Miriam, appreciate it." Rafe ran a hand through his short hair, then scratched absently at his beard. "Riley, round up the enforcers and come back here. I'll call Kyle. We need to talk about this."

An hour later, Dottie was serving heaping slices of hot apple pie and mugs of coffee to a room full of wolf shifters. Rafe just rolled his eyes and kept his thoughts to himself. He thought Dottie was part magician because he damn well knew he didn't have any apple pie in his house that morning. Rafe waited until everyone had settled in, then he threw out the million-dollar question.

"Since it's probably going to be a while before we get any answers from our guest, does anyone know what's going on with Tom Sanders' pack?"

Riley and Mark glanced at Thane, who set his plate on the coffee table.

"We all know Tom has a problem with his temper, but the way I hear it, he's getting out of control. The fella Miriam is tending isn't the only one, but he's probably luckier than the rest because he got dumped in our laps."

"We gonna pay a visit, Rafe?" Riley asked.

"Since someone made it my business, we most certainly will, but not just yet," Rafe replied. "I want to talk to our guest to find out what happened to him and what's going on in that pack. I'm not walking into another alpha's territory unless I have the full story." He gave everyone a stern look. "That goes for all of you. No one goes off half-cocked looking for Sanders. Am I clear?"

There were no arguments, not that Rafe expected any. His men were all solid, loyal, and for the most part, level-headed. They were wolf shifters, though, there would always be a wild side to them.

"Riley, Mark, Thane, I want y'all to keep an extra close eye on the perimeters. I can deal with taking in one injured man, but I don't want this to become a regular habit or a dumping ground."

He turned to the big man sitting in the rocking chair. Quiet as usual, Kyle Martin waited for instructions. His brother had always been like that, quiet, unassuming, and as lethal as they came. The man was a gentle giant until it was time to go to work, which made him the best beta Rafe could have asked for. The man had his back 24/7. There was never any doubt about his loyalty and devotion to his older brother.

"Kyle, for now, keep an ear to the ground. Anything you hear about that pack and their alpha; I need to know."

"I'm on it." Kyle rose with surprising grace for a man his size. He nodded to the others and left as quietly as he'd come in.

Later that evening, Rafe was walking around the compound. Everyone was settling in, and things were peaceful. He liked this time of night, engaging with the sounds of the forest—crickets chirping, frogs croaking in the nearby creek, and the occasional hoots of an owl. Usually, he would let his wolf run, but it would have to wait this time.

Seeing Miriam's lights still on, he headed that way, wanting to check on the injured man. He wouldn't rush the poor guy for answers, but his curiosity was piqued. If the man had done something to deserve punishment, it would be a totally different story, although Rafe couldn't think of any crime deserving of such harsh disciplinary action. Then again, he was nothing like Tom Sanders.

Rafe's dominance and strength were well known among other packs. He demanded discipline and loyalty from his people, but he was fair, always listening to both sides of an issue before deciding judgment.

He knocked once but opened the door quickly when he heard screams from within. Sprinting to the guest bedroom, Rafe found Miriam's two sons, Danny and Steve, trying to hold the injured man down without inflicting further damage. Miriam was trying to soothe the man, but it obviously wasn't working.

"What's going on?" Rafe asked as he tried to make sense of the scene.

"Trying to set his broken bones is all," Miriam grunted. "He won't be able to shift until I can get him back together again, then have time to heal." She wiped her brow with her sleeve. "Poor guy isn't cooperating."

"Let me see if I can help." Rafe stood over the injured man, letting his alpha power wash over him. Rafe knew he wouldn't get the full effect because he wasn't a part of the Crossroads pack, but he'd recognize the power of an alpha. Sure enough, the man relaxed, falling limply in Danny and Steve's arms. They laid him down, and Miriam quickly went about her job. Thirty minutes later, it was done.

"Thanks, Rafe. That power roll helped," Miriam said with a sigh of relief. "I gave him a shifter dose of sedative so he can rest, hopefully, through the night. He should be able to shift by morning if all goes well."

"Let's hope so," Rafe agreed. "I'll come back then. Maybe we can find out who he is and what exactly happened to him."

Next morning, Rafe walked into his kitchen to find Kyle wading through a stack of pancakes. He arched a brow as he fixed himself a mug of coffee.

"Don't worry, there's plenty," Dottie assured him.

"You sure?" He sat down, eyeing his brother. "How soon will you have to make a grocery run?"

"Same as usual, every two weeks." Dottie slipped a plate in front of Rafe. "Let me know if you want more. I fried the bacon crispy, just the way you like it."

"Thanks, Dottie."

Kyle picked up a slice of bacon, made eye contact with Rafe, and bit into the crispy slice with relish.

"Enjoying yourself?"

Kyle nodded and helped himself to another slice of bacon.

Rafe pointed at the plateful of bacon with his coffee mug. "You *will* leave me some."

Kyle shrugged. "Of course, Alpha."

"Why are you here?"

"Dottie cooks for you."

"I thought that little omega was taking care of you. What was her name? Oh, yeah, Alicia. What happened to her?"

"Busy."

Rafe set his mug on the table and stared at his brother. "That crap works on everyone but me. Talk."

Kyle wiped his mouth with a napkin, pushed his plate away, and drank the last of his coffee. Rafe glared at him through the whole process.

"Talked to a guy who's in with a pack member of the Plantation Wolves. Seems their alpha has been helping himself to all the women in the pack, mated ones as well. He's passing around the omegas like party favors, and they're not handling the merchandise gently."

"Any idea what started all this? Tom's always been rough around the edges, but I don't think he's ever gone this far."

"Ever hear of a drug called Moonburst?"

Rafe thought about it before answering slowly, "I've heard the name, but I'm not familiar with it."

"Seems to be making the rounds with the younger shifters, and it's already a problem with a few packs, especially in the larger cities. Somebody's been playing with animal sedatives and cutting it with a human drug called fentanyl. It's a lethal mix. If you survive the dose, you get a high that makes you think you're invincible. It's also known to be an aphrodisiac, which is how most get started on it."

"Sanders got a hold of this stuff?"

"That's what I'm hearing. He's been sharing with his top boys, and they've been partying hard for a while now. How they're all still alive is a wonder."

"I don't get it, but it looks like I'm gonna have to deal with the trash." Rafe shook his head, sighing heavily. "Want to walk with me to Miriam's? I want to see if our guest is able to shift and can answer a few questions."

Kyle gestured toward the door. "Lead the way."

CLAIMING MAGICK

———————

Madison Granger

Chapter 1

Havenport, 1935

"You promised! You pledged yourself to me, and now you think to break your vow?"

Sarah Murphy's blood ran cold. How could he do this to her after all this time? She hid her hands in the folds of her skirt to conceal the tremors. The room was suddenly hot, and she couldn't breathe.

"Sarah, be reasonable," Jeremy pleaded. He never moved from the center of the room, only stood there, watching her from a distance.

"Reasonable, is it?" Sarah screeched. "For five years, I have waited for you, listened to your promises and sweet words. Now, you want to call it off like I was never anything to you?" She wanted to throw herself at him, and rake out his eyes, but she faced him as his words cut her heart to shreds.

"She's my Fated Mate. I can't turn my back on her. She's the one I'm meant to be with."

"What about me? Am I nothing to you? What am I supposed to do now? I'll be the laughingstock of Havenport. I'll never be able to show my face again." She wouldn't be able to walk along the town's streets. They would stare and point, and she wouldn't be able to bear the shame.

"I care for you, but she's my mate," Jeremy pressed. Trying another tactic, he hurried on. "People forget quickly, Sarah. You're overreacting, surely."

Sarah slapped Jeremy. The sting burned her fingers, leaving a glaring red handprint on his freshly shaven face.

"Overreacting, indeed! You'll live to regret this decision, Jeremy Reed." How dare he choose a mangy dog over her, a young, beautiful, and powerful witch? He would live to rue this day!

"Please, Sarah! How was I to know Jenny would come into my life? I didn't plan any of it to work out this way." Jeremy covered his cheek with a shaky hand. "Don't do anything foolish or something you'll regret. I know how you are when you feel you've been slighted."

Sarah stared at him in shock. He had the nerve...

"Slighted? I may have been slighted?" Her laugh was bordering on hysterical, breaking off on a sob. "I can promise, anything I do to you I won't regret for a minute."

"You have to understand. I did it for the good of the pack." He held out a hand to her.

Sarah slapped his hand away. "The pack... always the pack." She spat the words back at him. "That's what this is truly about. You were never planning on making me your wife. The pack wouldn't accept a witch. Oh, no. Now that you are Alpha, you had to find a suitable wife, another wolf like you."

Jeremy tugged on his sleeves and adjusted his collar. Pulling his timepiece from his pocket, he glanced at his watch.

"I have to go, I have other business to attend. Once again, I'm sorry to have distressed you, but my mind is made up. I'm going to take Jenny as my mate. I wish you only the best."

Sarah watched him leave without another word. Her hopes and dreams were shattered, crumbling into dust to be blown away by the four winds. How would she hold her head up after word got out she'd been jilted? She'd be laughed at behind her back—and knowing most of the town's women, they wouldn't be that discreet, they would laugh in front of her. She wouldn't be able to endure it. She had to do something!

Wrapping a shawl around her shoulders, she ventured into the cool night. Looking up, she was reminded it was a full moon. The Lady's silver glow seemed unusually bright. Her magick would be strong. Sarah sniffed. She would use it to her advantage. Hurrying back inside, she gathered what she would need.

Sarah carefully crushed the herbs she'd gathered, mixing them in a small bowl. Lighting her candles, she dipped the flame into the herbs, watching them hiss and crackle. Raising her hands and her voice, she called upon the goddesses of wrath and vengeance.

For the cruelty and the pain,
you have brought to me,
I turn the tables three times three.
When dusk comes through,
bringing light to your deed,
my curse upon you and all your seed.

I say this spell tonight,
I am witch. I stand and fight.

It was done. Jeremy Reed and his line would diminish... slowly but surely.

Chapter 2

Havenport, Present Day

Rowan Murphy heard the bell tinkle over the door, then her cat, Jinx, hissed, and a familiar voice called out.

"Buster, come here! You bad boy, come to Mama right this instant!"

What a wonderful start to a morning, Mrs. Rogers and her designer dog, Buster. Rowan rolled her eyes. *How many times had she asked that woman to leave the dog at home?* Preparing for the inevitable, she hastily redid her messy bun, silver tendrils framing her face. Anxious amethyst eyes stared back at her in the oval office mirror.

The crash was expected. So were the flurry of fur and the hissing, spitting fury of her cat. What Rowan didn't expect was the amount of damage done in the short time it took to get to the chaos, grab Jinx, and fend off the pint-sized demon dog. Baskets of crystals lay scattered along the long counter and floor, a small display case holding small jars of ointments had been knocked over, glass containers rolling away or broken, and small bags of incense were everywhere. She barely caught the statue of the Morrigan before it crashed to the floor.

"Mrs. Rogers, what did I tell you about bringing Buster into the store?" Rowan desperately tried to keep her voice calm, with an arm around a hissing Jinx and the Morrigan in her other hand. She tried to keep a pleasant smile on her face, but this one particular patron was a true test of her patience, to say the least.

"Oh, Rowan, you know I can't leave Buster at home. He would be so lonely. Wouldn't you be lonely, Mama's little baby boy?" She rained kisses on the little dog, who stared defiantly at Rowan.

Rowan was mentally going through her spellbooks for something that would work on small, spoiled, ankle-biters when the owner caught her attention.

"Did the amulet come in yet, dear?"

"The amulet? Oh, yes, I have it locked away in my office. Give me a minute and I'll get it for you." Rowan hurried to her office, once again reminding herself this was the very reason she put up with Mrs. Rogers and her irritating dog. By herself, the woman spent enough money in her shop to keep it running. Rowan couldn't afford to offend, much less alienate, the older woman.

"You need to stop antagonizing that demon dog. Stay in here for a while," she fussed at Jinx as she set him free on the small loveseat. She went behind her desk to a framed picture on the wall, and with a practiced spin, Rowan opened the safe. Carefully removing the slender box, she removed the lid, making sure nothing had happened to the necklace. It had been locked in the safe, away from harm, but stranger things had happened before.

Bringing the antique amulet to the counter, she showed it to Mrs. Rogers for her approval.

"At last! I've wanted this for so long," she stage-whispered to Rowan as if it was a huge secret. "I never thought Mr. Rourke would ever give it up, and at such a bargain, too!"

A bargain, indeed! Rourke had doubled the price of the amulet before he parted with it. The man held no sentimental value to his pieces. *He's in it for the profit.* Placing the lid back on the box, Rowan slid it into a bag and wrote out the receipt, making sure she added in the damage to her supplies and shop.

Mrs. Rogers reached into her purse, a wallet stuffed with receipts and cards, pulled one out without even looking at it, and handed it to Rowan.

"I'll pay for the damage to your shop, of course."

She never met Rowan's stare, still busy cuddling her traumatized baby. The sale was approved, and Rowan did a mental fist pump. Rent was covered for this month and next. Of course, she would have to make more ointment to replace the ones destroyed, but this way, she'd been paid for them. Once the older woman, with Buster in tow, left the shop, Rowan looked upward, a smirk on her face, as she called out.

"You can come out now. The coast is clear, and you both have cleanup duty."

A young woman with flaming-red, spiral curls and green eyes slipped into the room, quietly joined by a young man with a mop of unruly black hair and crystal blue eyes. Amy and Jason, Rowan's shop assistants, showed a lot of potential except when it came to dealing with the more difficult customers, like Mrs. Rogers. Then they whipped out their invisible capes, and she was on her own.

"Sorry, Ro, but I was in the bathroom," Amy apologized with a giggle. "Some things can't be rushed."

Rowan arched a brow in Jason's direction.

"In my defense, I was in the back, unpacking boxes," Jason declared. "You were already dealing with her before I even knew she was here."

"You are both in the clear... this time." Rowan sighed. "But you need to learn how to deal with these women. As unpleasant as they and their animals are, they keep us afloat, and thanks to today's sale, we're floating quite nicely," she said with a smile, her irritation with the situation lifting instantly.

"Did someone say pizza?" Jason favored her with his best lopsided grin.

"I don't recall saying anything at all about food." Rowan laughed in spite of herself. "But I think we can manage a pizza for lunch."

"I want pineapple!" Amy called dibs.

"You had it last time," Jason complained.

"You two work it out. One pizza only," she warned. "I have work to do in my office. Clean up that disaster and try to keep the place intact and running."

"Yes, ma'am," Amy and Jason chorused.

Rowan sat at her desk, staring at the desktop screen for a moment. Her wallpaper was a photo taken when she was a child. It was a shot of her grandparent's house on a hazy summer day, with a rope swing hung from an old oak in the front yard. If you looked past the house, you could make out the barn in the back. She missed it all—her grandparents, the house, the horses.

She'd had a memorable childhood, and it stemmed from that one place. She blew her bangs up in a huff. It was all gone now. The only thing keeping her going was her dream that one day she would buy back the piece of property her grandfather had sold. It wouldn't bring her childhood, or her grandparents back, but she wanted the house and the land. It had sentimental value. A piece of her heart was there, and it was all she wanted.

Rowan sat back, looking out the window at nothing. She needed to take the picture down and bury those memories. Every day, she saw the picture, and it was the same thing—pleasant memories, a yearning wish for what once was, and more fuel to the hatred burning in her heart. It was eating her alive, and the worst part was she knew it, and it truly wasn't justified.

It wasn't their fault, not really. They bought the land. She shouldn't hate them, but she did. She hated the shifters for taking what should have been hers.

About the Author

Madison Granger is a free-spirited late bloomer. She stubbornly lives by three beliefs: dreams can come true, never give up, and you're never too old to try new things. She is living proof of all three adages, vowing she isn't done by a long shot.

Born and raised near New Orleans and even closer to the swamps of south Louisiana, Madison is no stranger to tales of the magical and different.

Madison loves to read, listen to music (mostly country, with a little alternative thrown in), thrives on coffee, and has had a life-long love of horses. She collects dragons, gargoyles, and angels... and anything else that catches her fancy.

Madison's stories are touched by magic, revolving around sexy Alphas, curvy, strong-willed heroines, and they always have a Happy Ever After.

Madison welcomes stalkers... well, the book kind anyway, and would love for you to join her journey.

Website
https://www.MadisonGranger.com/

Facebook
https://www.facebook.com/MadisonGrangerAuthor/

Readers Group
https://www.facebook.com/groups/2886808738200587

Instagram
https://www.instagram.com/madisongrangerauthor/

TikTok
https://www.tiktok.com/@madisongrangerauthor

MeWe
https://mewe.com/myworld

Milton Keynes UK
Ingram Content Group UK Ltd.
UKHW020818280823
427620UK00015B/793